CHANGE OF HEART

An LDS Novel

Also by Roseanne E. Wilkins

Tangled Hearts: An LDS Novel
Hidden in the Heart: An LDS Novel

Noonday Sun: A Fanfiction Book

Children's Fiction:

The Fruitful Tree

CHANGE OF HEART

An LDS Novel

Roseanne Evans Wilkins

Change of Heart: An LDS Novel
Copyright © 2012
Roseanne Evans Wilkins
Saluki Press

Cover Design by Create Space
Cover Photograph by David P. Smith/Shutterstock

Printed in the United States of America
Charleston, South Carolina

ISBN-13: 978-1-4609-6025-7
ISBN-10: 1-4609-6025-4

Cataloging Data
Wilkins, Roseanne Evans
  Change of Heart: an LDS Novel / by Roseanne Evans Wilkins
      p. cm. - (Kansas Connections)
ISBN 1-4609-6025-4 (pbk.)
{1. LDS Romance — Fiction. 2. LDS Suspense — Fiction.
        3. Kansas (State) — Fiction}
I. Title. II. Series: Wilkins, Roseanne Evans. Kansas Connections.

To Liesel Augis
and to my wonderful grandmother,
Lola C. Evans

ACKNOWLEDGEMENTS

Thanks to all my beta readers who spent their valuable time reading over my manuscript: Beth, Jennie, Karen, Krista, Nicole, Noreen, Rhonda, and Tamra. Thanks also to my children for giving up some "Mom time" and for enduring some interesting meals during the process. Thanks to Craig for supporting me in jumping into the new territory of authorship and for being my editor. It's been an exciting ride for both of us.

Table of Contents

Roseanne Evans Wilkins

Prologue

Takeshi Yukiko, his white jacket pristine, stared through the bars of the small cage. He watched the rabbit crawl to the feeding tray and start to nibble on the fresh lettuce, unaffected by the heavy panting of its companion.

Takeshi looked up as Yasanari Yokichi joined him in observing the rabbits. She glanced at the face of her gold watch. The diamonds flashed as she moved. "The antidote was administered 60 minutes ago?" Her words were clipped and assured.

Takeshi nodded, unable to hide the pleased smile that spread across his face. "One hour. Look at the difference."

They both watched the two rabbits. The first was happily nibbling on the lettuce, her open wounds quickly sealing shut. The other lay prone on the floor, her skin gaping awkwardly in various stages of sloughing. The wounds did not bleed. They merely continued to open, eaten alive by the yeast that devoured her living body.

Yasanari nodded then picked up her phone. "The first subject shows excellent results. How do you want to proceed?" She listened briefly and shut her phone. "You are to administer the antidote to the remaining rabbits, except for this one." She thrust her chin at the ailing animal panting in the cage. "I need a full write up on the results on my desk in the morning."

Takeshi was filling a needle as she spoke. "You can count on it." His voice was a pleased purr.

Chapter 1, BYU

Christina

"I love you, Dad. Tell Mom and everyone else at home that I love them and miss them already." My farewell hug was fierce. I didn't want to let go.

"I will. Don't worry. Take care of yourself, and be sure to call if you need anything." Dad returned my hug then headed into the Salt Lake Airport Terminal.

I wiped away a tear threatening to wander its way down my cheek. The intensity of my feelings surprised me. Watching Dad walk away was like watching my childhood disappear. As much as I wanted to attend BYU, leaving Salina wasn't as easy as I thought it would be.

When one of the airport security guards headed my way on his personal hovercraft, I hurried to climb back into the new-to-me compact car. I didn't need a ticket to add to my growing list of expenses.

With one last look at the airport doors, I checked over my shoulder for coming traffic and merged into the crowded lane.

All my attention went to navigating south I-15 through Salt Lake City. My older car didn't have the automatic navigation of all the newer models, so merging into the heavy traffic took all my concentration. After I drove past Point of the Mountain and traffic thinned, I tried to review all the purchases that still needed to be made. Since I was living in on-campus housing, I didn't have to buy any apartment essentials, but I still had to buy my own bedding and towels. The old dorms had been replaced with streamlined versions where each dorm held two students, a couple of single beds, and an attached bathroom. All the meals were expected to be eaten in the cafeteria.

Mom wanted to send the bedding and towels with me, but I reminded her the car was a compact and wouldn't fit much more than the wardrobe I planned to pack. Dad had driven with me to Provo so we could switch off driving. I was grateful for his company. Driving so far alone wasn't on my bucket list.

It was almost 4:00 p.m. when I arrived at the dormitories after dropping off Dad. The new underground parking required a pass code to enter, and the safety feature thrilled my parents. There had been too many muggings over the years near the women's dorms. They didn't want me added to the statistics.

I pulled into the parking entrance and entered the code. The metal door opened with a sigh. This wasn't like any other parking garage I'd used. It was meant to keep walking traffic out.

As I pulled into my assigned parking stall, the bright overhead lights were a relief. No dark corners for predators to hide in. I shuddered. My own birth father had been a predator. I shut the door on that dark thought as I slammed the door of my car.

Dad and I had delivered my luggage to the room earlier that day, so I had one thing on my agenda. Shopping. In a big family, it wasn't often I got to spend money. This was one of those times, and I smiled in anticipation, backpack ready to go.

It only took a few minutes to walk to the Wilkinson Center. The clatter of dishes on trays reminded me that I hadn't eaten dinner yet. The CougarEat was full of arriving students. My stomach growled warningly, but I wanted to get my books purchased and delivered to my dorm. I'd heard horror stories about students not being able to get needed textbooks, and I didn't want to be one of those students.

As I entered the crowded bookstore, I worked my way over to wide stairs leading to the second floor. I grabbed the railing and tried to avoid the crowd as I walked up the stairs. As much as I disliked crowds, I couldn't help feeling thrilled at the sight of so many members of the church in one place. After growing up in Salina where I was the only member in my entire high school class, I couldn't help but be moved.

When I reached the second floor, I stepped outside the stream of traffic and scanned the room for an employee. I spotted a petite redhead in a store tunic. One student had just stepped away. Another had already taken his place. I scurried over, anxious for assistance of my own. When the redhead turned to me, I asked, "Can you tell me how I can find these books?"

She looked over my list. "The numbers next to the books are found on the shelves. They're arranged numerically. You should be able to find them. I don't think any are out of stock at the moment."

I nodded. "Thanks for your help." I felt foolish for asking such an obvious question, but all this was new to me. I had no idea what I was doing.

When I'd loaded all my textbooks into my arms, I worked my way to one of the long lines leading to a checkout. My arms were shaking with fatigue by the time I reached the clerk. The blond clerk didn't even look up as I dropped the books on the counter. She grabbed the top book and ran it through the scanner. She looked as tired as I did. *How long has she been ringing up loads of textbooks?* I wondered

Despite her fatigued appearance, she was efficient. It only took a couple of minutes for her to run the books through the scanner. I swallowed a gasp as the total rang up. Dad had said textbooks were expensive. He hadn't been kidding. I tried to do the math to figure out how much I had left for pleasure shopping, but my tired brain wouldn't function. I'd have to wait and do the figuring when I could find a quiet corner to work my calculator. At the head of a long line of grumpy students wasn't the place.

"Thanks," I mumbled.

Her smile was half-hearted as she gazed past me to take in the never-ending line of students. "Have a nice day," she managed through her frozen smile.

I breathed a sigh of relief as I shoved the books into my backpack. At least they fit. I shouldered the heavy load and headed back down the stairs into the main bookstore— the non-textbook part. It had been a while since I'd shopped in a real bookstore. The smell of print on paper was heady. Most reading in the world had long since passed over to ebooks, but BYU still had a bookstore. I stopped at a bookshelf and thumbed through a few books. The tactile experience was something I always enjoyed. The touch and smell of print on paper just couldn't be reproduced on a reader.

Mom and Dad had an extensive library at home. They hadn't ever gone over to the ebook readers, so I grew up surrounded by print books. They even had two complete sets of encyclopedias. My fellow classmates just didn't know what they were missing. There was something about flipping through an encyclopedia to find information and then getting sidetracked by a different topic. "Accidental learning" was what my mom called it. I called it fun.

As I thumbed through a book on the life of Christ, I jumped when I felt a tap on my shoulder.

"Excuse me. I think this is yours."

I looked up at the owner of the voice. He had dark curly hair and warm brown eyes. *Wow,* I thought, *I didn't know brown eyes could twinkle.*

I'd grown up surrounded by blue and hazel eyes. I'd never had much interaction with brown ones. *Do my eyes twinkle like that?* I wondered.

His eyes mesmerized me, but his voice broke into my thoughts.

Confused, I stared at a copy of *Days of Awe* by Gale Boyd. It was required reading for the Book of Mormon class.

"Umm...where did you find it?"

"You were standing in front of me upstairs. It must've fallen off your stack of books. I didn't notice I had an extra book until after the clerk rang up the transaction."

"I'm so sorry." I reached for the book to put it in with my other books then dropped my backpack. "Let me pay you back." I pulled several books out. "I know my wallet is in here somewhere." As I dug through the backpack, I was trying to remember how much cash I had on hand. I didn't normally carry more than a few dollars because I usually did all my purchases with an ATM card. As I was digging through the backpack, my stomach let out a tell-tale gurgle. A flush ran up my face.

The tall stranger grinned down at me. "Sounds like you're hungry." He held out his hand to help me up. I stared at it in confusion. My wallet was still missing.

I couldn't lie. My stomach wouldn't let me. I stuffed the books back in the bag then reached for his hand and grinned as I stood. "Yeah. I just wanted to get my books bought before I ate."

"Mother always told me to never shop on an empty stomach," he informed me.

"I thought that was only grocery shopping."

His expression was serious, but amusement showed in his eyes. "Mother said it's hard to think straight on an empty stomach. Let's go remedy your situation. My treat."

He must've seen the indecision on my face, because he continued, "I'm Todd. Todd Cohen, by the way. Aren't you Christina Andrews?"

My eyes widened with shock. I glanced down at my dark blue polo to see if I'd forgotten to remove a name tag I didn't know existed.

Todd chuckled at my obvious confusion. "My sister is Nan Cohen. I believe she's your roommate."

"Yes, she is." My brow furrowed. "How did you know me?"

"Your picture is in her registration packet. I was curious to see who her roommate was."

I remembered some kind of picture included with my packet. It was a security feature so we'd recognize our roommates, but I hadn't paid much attention. I tried to scan my brain for the image. All that came back was a hazy picture of someone about my age with dark hair in a short A-line bob. Her brown eyes had matched my own, but I hadn't studied the photograph enough to memorize her features.

"I have to admit that I was at a loss for words when you were standing in front of me in line. I couldn't think how I could introduce myself without sounding like some kind of stalker." He laughed at himself. "I figure the cost of your book is a small price to pay to give me a reason to introduce myself."

Knowing he was my roommate's brother helped me relax. With my past, I was hesitant to interact with strangers.

Todd continued, "I saw how many books you were carrying. Your bag's got to weigh a ton. Can I pack it for you?"

My eyes were in a permanent wide stare. Shock was the operative word. I didn't argue as he picked up my backpack. My arms were fatigued from holding the books in line, and packing them on my back hadn't been much better.

"Do you mind if we stop at the CougarEat?" he asked.

I shook my head, still speechless, and followed him to the cafeteria. At least I could blink. Maybe I'd start breathing in a minute.

As we walked through the line, I relaxed enough to be able to look over the food offerings. When we reached the head of the line, I listened while Todd ordered his food. Dad had told me I should wait and let the guy order first so I would have a price guideline to follow. After Todd placed his order, I stepped up to the counter. "I'll have a Caesar grilled chicken salad with lemonade as the drink, and I'd like the honey mustard salad dressing to go with it." The clerk behind the counter looked up in surprise, but nodded and reached for the proper packet of dressing.

Todd led me to a secluded table at the back of the noisy room. I was surprised he could find anything remotely private with the crowd at the eatery. He settled my backpack full of textbooks on the floor between our two chairs. His own bulging backpack rested next to mine.

When we sat down to eat, I examined his features. I was trying to remember how Nan looked and if they shared a family resemblance. I stifled a sigh. *If only I'd studied her picture.*

Before he took a bite of his cheeseburger, he asked, "So have you decided on a major?"

I shook my head. "Not yet. I'm wavering between several options."

He nodded. "No need to tie yourself down. You'll have plenty of time to decide."

9

"Yeah. That's what I think." I reached for the honey mustard dressing, tore open the packet, and drizzled the dressing over the salad. The blend of spicy sweet honey mustard combined with the scent of broiled chicken made my mouth water. Before my stomach could give off another embarrassing gurgle, I dug into the salad.

Todd and I were both quiet for the next few minutes while we enjoyed our meals.

I searched my brain for some kind of safe topic. "So, how long have you been attending BYU?"

"I attended before my mission and then came back after. I split my time between the campus in Israel and here."

My eyes widened in surprise. "I didn't know there was a campus in Israel."

"It's not always open to students outside of Israel, but it's open for the study abroad students when it's considered safe."

I tried to figure out how this information applied to Todd. "So. . . are you from Israel?"

"Yes. My parents live there. I'll be finished with my classes in December. I'll come back for graduation in the spring. I can accompany Nan back to Israel then."

My brows furrowed in question. "So how did you end up attending BYU?"

"Mother attended BYU. It has one of the best accounting schools in the United States. She converted to the church while she was attending. My parents were already married then. Father never did convert, but he didn't forbid her membership."

"Wow. That must've been tough."

"In some ways, but I believe events in our lives are always for a reason. I was able to see how the ancient traditions enhance understanding of LDS religious practices." He paused and leaned over to tap my backpack.

10

"Days of Awe teaches a lot of what I grew up with. I'm not surprised it's required reading now. I'm sure you'll find it fascinating."

After I finished, I pushed back from the table. "That was delicious. Thanks for dinner."

"My pleasure." Todd grinned at me. "I'd like to do this again sometime."

What? Why would he want to see me again? We hardly talked. "Um...yeah...so would I." My response sounded hesitant, even to me.

"Can I add your number to my cell phone?"

"I...I guess so." I tried to think of some reason why he shouldn't have my phone number. *It's not like he can trace me on it. Dad always makes sure our phones don't have that ability. Besides, if he really is Nan's brother, he already knows exactly where I live.* I rattled off my phone number.

"Would you like me to walk you home?"

"Um...sure. Okay, I guess."

Todd bent to retrieve the backpacks and threw them over his shoulder with practiced ease.

As we headed out the door toward the familiar dorms, I asked, "Do you have any other siblings?"

He shook his head and looked down at me. "No. I only have a sister." He paused a moment, as if weighing his next question with care. "How many brothers and sisters do you have?"

"I have three brothers and two sisters."

"Nice."

"Yeah. Our big family is a lot of fun."

"I'll bet."

Curious, I asked, "What's your major?"

"I'm finishing my Masters in Accounting."

Masters? Wow. He's got to be years older than me. Why would he even be interested in a lowly freshman?

11

Then I remembered Dad saying the returned missionaries seemed to make a beeline for the freshmen women. *Beeline, indeed. I've only been here one day!* I glanced up at Todd. *Which reminds me…*

"So where did you serve your mission?"

"I served in Japan."

"Was it hard to learn the language?"

He chuckled. "Total immersion teaches a language fast."

"I'll bet." I bit my bottom lip. "I'm worried about my Spanish class. I'm sure there will be some returned missionaries attending. Even though I took it in high school, it isn't the same as a total immersion experience."

Todd grinned. "I doubt the returned missionaries are taking the class to learn the language. It's just an easy grade."

I shuddered. "It won't be an easy grade for me. I'm not looking forward to the competition."

"I'm sure you'll do fine." Todd tried to reassure me. "Not all the students are returned missionaries. Isn't it Spanish one?" I nodded, and he continued. "The Spanish one class shouldn't have many returned missionaries, anyway. Most of them test out of that class and move on to the higher levels. It gives them an easy credit."

His reassurance made me feel better, but I was still worried about it. I changed the subject. "How long have you been back?"

"A couple of years."

"Have you been at BYU the whole time?"

"As I mentioned before, I've split my time between the two campuses. The majority of the accounting classes are only offered here in Provo."

I nodded as if I understood. "So you need one more semester?"

"Yes. Then it's back to Israel."

"Do you have a job there?"

"My family owns an accounting firm. I was planning to work with my parents."

Our conversation came to an abrupt halt as Todd opened the heavy glass doors to the dormitory. He handed back my heavy backpack. "Here. I'd like to carry it to your room for you, but I'm not allowed past the front lobby."

"Thanks for packing it for me." I wasn't quite sure what to say to him. *Should I ask if we'll meet again?* I clamped my teeth shut. How did the saying go? *It is better to remain silent and be thought a fool than to open one's mouth and remove all doubt. Wasn't it Abraham Lincoln who said that?*

My musings were interrupted by Todd. "I'll be in touch."

"Okay." I added softly, "Thanks for the book and dinner."

He grinned and winked at me. "My pleasure." Then he was gone, the spicy scent of an unknown fragrance coloring the air he'd just vacated. I breathed it in then headed up to my room.

Roseanne Evans Wilkins

Chapter 2, Nan

As I entered the small dorm room, I was happy it was still empty. I expected Nan to be there—especially since I'd just met her brother.

I dropped the heavy backpack on the naked bed I'd chosen for myself. I sighed. My meeting with Todd was so overwhelming that I'd forgotten I needed to pick up my bedding. I scanned the room, making sure my personal belongings were properly stowed. When Dad and I had dropped off my things earlier, I'd picked my side of the room and my closet space. Hopefully, Nan wouldn't mind. *If she's anything like her brother, I have nothing to worry about.*

As I suspected earlier, my wallet had worked its way down to the bottom of my backpack. The textbooks were soon stacked on the tiny corner desk area. I left the other desk empty. After transferring my wallet to my purse, I stepped out of the room and made sure the door was locked.

A few minutes later, I was in my car waiting for the garage doors to open. A small flashy sports car entered the garage as I was leaving. I had a vague impression that the dark-haired female in the driver's seat looked familiar. Her chic short hair was the height of fashion. I tossed my own long dark tresses over my shoulder almost self-consciously. I wondered if the driver was Nan. I shrugged. I would know soon enough.

It didn't take long to drive to the nearest mall. I spent a few minutes picking through bedding and towels. My budget wouldn't let me go extravagant, so choices were limited. At least I found something in colors I liked. As I reached for the brilliant blues, I wondered about Nan. What if our color choices clashed? Would she care?

Reluctantly, I turned from the colors I loved to the whites and blacks. *Solid black is way too depressing. The white eyelet is pretty but it seems young for a college student.* I chose a bold black and white geometric pattern for the comforter with plain white sheets to match. *The black and white will probably keep its fresh look. White towels can bleach clean.*

Satisfied with my choices, I headed to the checkout counter. This shopping trip had been more invigorating than the textbook shopping, and the bedding was bulky but not nearly as heavy. I placed my load on the counter. The male clerk at the register was a little taller than Dad. Six foot six maybe. His blue eyes complimented his white-blond hair, and a dimple in his right cheek appeared when he smiled. I couldn't help smiling in return.

"Did you find everything you needed?" His delicious baritone sent chills up my arms. It was a pleasure to hear him talk.

I nodded.

He glanced up at me as he ran my purchases through the scanner. "Are you attending school here?"

I nodded again. "BYU." I paused, then asked, "You?"

"Yeah. I'm attending UVU."

"Really? That's where my mom graduated. What's your major?"

"Secondary Education with an emphasis in history."

"Wow. Sounds…interesting." *I would've never guessed education,* I mused.

"Say. . . there's a dance Friday night on campus. How would you like to go with me?"

Yikes. I can't even pretend I know this guy. What do I say? I glanced at his name badge, where Henry was clearly stamped. Without realizing I'd said anything, I blurted out "Sounds fun." Horror welled up inside me. *Tell me I didn't just say I'd go out with a complete stranger. Dad is going to kill me...that is, if Henry doesn't.* I looked up into his clear blue eyes and decided I would be safe at a campus event.

"Can I have your phone number?"

I stared at him blankly.

"So I can make arrangements to pick you up," he clarified.

"Oh. Okay. Sure." I rattled off my number while he added it to his own cell phone.

I suppressed a shudder as I packed up my purchases and left. Hopefully, the date with Henry would go as well as the date with Todd. I had more requests for dates in one day than I'd had my entire high school career. I'd had to ask out my date for senior prom. The only guy my age in the ward had been too shy to ask me out himself.

As I entered my dorm room a few minutes later loaded with packages, I wasn't surprised to see the driver of the flashy sports car. She had put her bed together with the same kind of white eyelet I'd rejected as looking too immature. *It does look pretty.* I admitted. *I hope my bedding won't clash with the eyelet. I hadn't thought about styles. Ugh.*

I dropped my packages on the bed and tried to hide my anxiety as I approached Nan, who looked up from her writing. "Hi. My name is Christina." I offered my hand.

Nan stood to administer a firm shake. "I'm Nan." Her smile revealed brilliantly white teeth. *Recently whitened.* I found myself thinking, but immediately regretted the

17

thought. She seemed as genuine as Todd. "My brother told me all about you."

I laughed. "I hope it was all good."

She nodded. "He said we'd get along well. I'm glad."

"Me, too." I turned to my packages and made my bed. *Mom would be horrified to know I didn't wash my sheets before using them, but what Mom doesn't know. . .* I swallowed a chuckle as I pictured her face. I folded and put away the few towels I'd bought then returned and dropped, sitting cross legged in the middle of the bed.

Nan had already returned to her writing. She looked up as I sat down. "So. . . this is your first year?"

I nodded. "Yours, too?"

Nan echoed my nod. "I'm majoring in business administration. Have you picked a major?"

I shook my head. "No. I wanted to take a few general education classes before I make up my mind."

Nan turned back to her writing. I stared at her bent head a few seconds then focused on the view outside the window. All I could see was the side of "Y" mountain. The summer had taken its toll. The aspen leaves were the brownish side of green, and any grass was a withered straw yellow. Even the few visible pines looked dry. Only the silver gray sagebrush seemed unaffected by the heat.

I stifled a sigh. I wanted a talkative roommate— especially since I'd been out with her brother. I thought we'd have a lot to talk about.

The textbooks beckoned. It wouldn't hurt to go through my syllabuses and thumb through the reading material. *Maybe having a studious roommate will be a blessing.* I stood up and moved over to the desk.

I was soon immersed in looking over the material and hardly noticed when Nan got dressed for bed.

"Would you like to join me in prayer?" Nan's quiet request was a shock. I hadn't even thought about having prayer with my roommate.

"Uh…sure." I mumbled and knelt next to my bed while she knelt next to hers.

"Do you want to offer, or shall I?"

Unsure of what to say in a roommate prayer, I answered. "You go ahead."

Her simple prayer sounded much like the prayers I'd offered for my family in Salina. She mentioned the prophet and missionaries and her family and mine. As she climbed into bed, my heart filled with gratitude. *What other place on earth would offer me an LDS roommate who felt perfectly natural asking me to participate in family prayer?*

I took my turn in the bathroom and pulled on the brilliant green pajamas Mom had bought before I left. I loved how the color offset my dark hair and brown eyes— not that I had any intention of ever entertaining in them. I blushed at the thought.

Their long legs and long sleeves with tailored collar were modest enough, but the silk material followed my curves in too many places. I suddenly wished for the robe Mom had packed with my things. I'd never bothered with a robe before since my bedtime attire had always been worn old sweats coupled with long t-shirts. Tailored pajamas were not something I was accustomed to.

Relief washed over me as I remembered Nan had already climbed into her own bed. The robe wasn't necessary. My bare feet were silent as I moved to my bed.

Staring at the ceiling, I listened to Nan's regular breathing. She wasn't sharing the same struggle to sleep I was. Images of my family waving good-bye and Dad heading all alone into the airport terminal brought tears to my eyes. I hadn't realized how homesick I would be. I was so excited to start this new adventure. The ache from missing my family was a surprise.

My thoughts turned to happier events. As I thought of my meeting with Todd, my lips curved into a smile. He'd been like a solicitous brother—the big brother I'd never had.

Then my mind turned to Henry's blue eyes and white blond hair. With his image on my mind, I rolled over and fell asleep.

The next morning, I found myself at the Administration Building checking out the job board. I'd taken some business classes that might qualify me for some kind of administrative work.

As I was waiting at a table for my name to be called, I picked up a stray copy of *The Deseret News*. I flipped through the "A" section, and a small article caught my eye.

"Chinese Two-Child Rule Impacts Japanese Mafia." I scanned through the article. I already knew China had revoked its one-child rule. They'd figured out that a 150/100 male/female child population wasn't good for the health of their country.

During the height of the "one child" rule, the Japanese Mafia had smuggled unwanted Chinese girls out of China to service the red-light districts in Japan. Japanese ties to the sex slave industry had been an embarrassment to civilized countries for years.

According to the article, the Japanese Mafia had increased their presence in the more lucrative business of providing arms to both sides of the Israeli conflict.

As I was perusing the article, I caught a whiff of a familiar scent and looked up. "Hi, Todd." I couldn't hide my welcoming smile. "What are you doing here?"

He dropped into the seat next to mine with a weary sigh. "I could ask you the same thing, but I'll answer you first." He ran frustrated fingers through his tousled hair. "I'm trying to help Nan adjust her schedule. She took too many classes. This is her first semester. She didn't realize how difficult carrying 24 credits could be."

"Twenty-four. Wow. How come she took so many?"

He chuckled. "She thinks she's super woman, I guess. I finally talked her into dropping one of the math classes."

"She'll probably thank you for it later." I looked up as my name was called.

"I'm applying for some assistant secretarial positions." I whispered. "Wish me luck."

"Good luck. I hope you get the one you want."

"I'd be happy with anything at the moment." I grinned at him. "Thanks."

With Todd's warm smile of encouragement filling my mind, I walked through the office door with calm confidence.

Savannah's name plate was displayed on her desk. Her easy manner kept me relaxed, and I was able to answer her questions with confidence. At the end of the interview, I stood up and shook her hand.

"You'll be hearing back from us by the end of the week."

"Thanks." I smiled back at her. "I'm looking forward to it."

As I stepped into the waiting area, Todd glanced up from a copy of the student newspaper he'd been reading. He smiled a greeting. "How'd it go?"

Wrinkling my nose at him, I shrugged. "I thought it went well, but I'll hear her point of view in a couple of days."

"Want to get a celebratory smoothie?" He placed the newspaper on the table as he stood.

"It's a little early for celebrating, but a smoothie sounds nice."

Todd didn't offer his hand and I didn't reach for his. It felt too much like a big brother taking me for a treat. *He has plenty of things to do with his time. He doesn't need to be babysitting his sister's roommate, but it's sooo sweet.*

The August sun beat down on us as we walked to the Wilkinson Center. Colorful splashes of flowers nodded to a hot summer breeze.

"How is your family?" Todd asked.

"All the kids are getting ready for school."

"Where do you fit in the family?"

"I'm the oldest."

Todd glanced down and caught my gaze. "How is your mother doing without you?"

My brows grew together in a puzzled frown. "She's coping, but she says she misses me. Why do you ask?"

He stepped forward to open the heavy glass door of the bookstore as he answered. "From the article I just read, it sounds like you were very involved with your siblings."

My eyes went wide in shock. "What article?"

He chuckled at my obvious surprise. "There was a short bio on all the Presidential Scholars. You and Nan were included."

"Oof. I didn't realize the bios were going to be published in the student paper." My face warmed with embarrassment. "I should've known Nan had earned a scholarship, too."

"You were assigned as roommates because of your scholarships."

I stepped inside the building before anyone complained about the open door. The heat was already causing a few stray glances our way.

"I didn't realize…" Chagrined, I wondered how much of the roommate packet I had missed. It was true that I hadn't done more than glance over it. I should have done a more thorough perusal.

We cut through the bookstore and down the hall to the steps that led to the bottom floor. I hesitated a moment at the top of the stairs. Marble open stairs. Ugh. I glanced down at my sensible flats. *Perfect choice for treading up and down staircases.*

Todd noticed my slight hesitation. He raised an eyebrow in a silent question, and I moved to follow him without explaining. *I'm not sure what my fear of staircases means, and I'm not going to open myself to psychological evaluation. I got enough of that from my dad.* I felt a rush of guilt at the thought and amended, *Not that he ever used his profession against me. He was careful not to be obvious about it.* I followed Todd to the smoothie shop nestled next to the theatre.

We talked about the weather and the possibility of the football team producing another Heisman winner while we waited for our orders. After our drinks were delivered, we walked back up the stairs to find an empty table.

When we were settled, Todd asked, "So what led you to working with a therapy dog?"

I dropped my gaze and traced a line through the frost on the outside of my glass. "Dad is a therapist. We received a Great Dane from one of his patients." I glanced up at Todd. "Peppy has one ear that won't stand up, so he couldn't make it in the show ring. His official coloring is Harlequin, but I can't help thinking clownish pirate. The eye closest to his floppy ear is covered with a black spot." Todd smiled at the description, and I continued. "Peppy is so good with people Dad thought I'd enjoy taking him to nursing homes. There are a couple in Salina. He did so well there that I branched out into the neighboring communities." I could hear the enthusiasm in my voice and wondered if Todd would understand. "He worked especially well with the Veterans."

Todd seemed genuinely interested. "What does a therapy dog do?"

I chuckled. "He mostly just gets petted and talked to. He loves it."

"Who takes him now?"

"Funny you should ask." I paused and looked up to watch some passing students then glanced back at Todd. "Dad works with kids who have Reactive Attachment Disorder. He thought it would help the teenagers with the disorder to reach out and help others. He picked a few he felt would benefit the most and is planning to take them one at a time to the nursing homes."

"How is that working out?"

"Tomorrow will be the first day." I paused a moment and caught Todd's eyes. "I have to admit I'm feeling a little jealous. It was one of my favorite activities."

"Sounds. . . rewarding." Todd's mesmerizing look left me breathless. After a few silent moments, Todd seemed to withdraw and glanced at his watch. "I have an appointment I can't miss." When his eyes met mine again, I could see a question there. His brown eyes were easy to read. "Would you like to come with Nan and me to the first fireside of the fall semester?"

"I'd love to." I agreed. "I'll get with Nan on the details." Todd stood and picked up his empty glass and reached for mine. He had them both bussed before I had a chance to stand.

I watched as he headed out the glass doors. *I know he wouldn't have met me without Nan, but I wonder if our relationship would have been different without his little sister as a link.* I sighed and scooted my chair back to leave. *I can't imagine he sees me as anything but his sister's roommate.*

Classes didn't start until the following week. With no pressing appointments, I meandered back to the dorms. I wasn't hungry after the tall drink, so I didn't feel the need to stop at the cafeteria for lunch.

When I reached my room, I opened my laptop and checked my email. It took a couple of minutes to answer the small number of notes from family and friends.

As I sat and stared at the screen, the realization hit me that I could finally open my own Facebook account. Mom and Dad would never let me while I was living at home, but I wasn't living at home any more.

Within minutes, my account was up and running. I sent a friend request to my mom. Dad had a fanpage I "liked." Then I added the friends who had always used Mom's account to chat with me.

Feeling brave at my achievement toward independent adult status, I clicked on the Twitter login page. My parents had never had Twitter accounts. Maybe it had something to do with their holding out against ebook readers. Whatever it was, I wasn't under their roof any more, and I could certainly choose whether or not I was going to Twitter.

I stared at the screen a moment and tried to think of a clever user name. I wanted something that wouldn't give me away as a single female. Mom and Dad had instilled the need for caution at an early age. Knowing the story behind my conception led me to understand their anxiety.

Carpe Diem. It was a Latin term meaning seize the day. Seemed clever enough, but I wanted something even more different. Something original. Everyone had heard Carpe Diem at one time or another. I stared at the screen another moment and thought about Todd.

He had gone to Japan on his mission. Wouldn't it be different to choose a Japanese name? Maybe Carpe Diem translated into Japanese? I used Google translate and came up with my handle, a series of characters that looked like a number seven with a hat on top, a crossed small "t" over a small "c," a pagoda with a bird on the left, a "c" with an antenna stuck on top, and a fancy "3." I had no idea if I got the translation right, but I trusted the translation site. My laptop had a standard-issue international keyboard.

Satisfied I had an original handle, I filled in the pertinent information and opened my Twitter account. I found a friend I knew from high school and followed all her friends. Next, I posted a link to the article I'd read earlier on the Japanese Mafia in Israel since I thought it was fascinating and then logged out. I'd wasted enough time on the internet already.

The next few days were a whirlwind of activity. I almost forgot about the dance with Henry. When I saw an unfamiliar number flash on my cell phone, I debated about whether or not to pick it up then remembered it might be him. "Hello?"

I recognized his mesmerizing voice when he answered me. "Hi. This is Henry. I was calling about the dance tomorrow night. Did you want to go anywhere before?"

I bit my lip, *Do I want to spend more time with Henry? He is a stranger, after all.* "I have plans for dinner." I answered. "What time does the dance start?"

"8:00. Can I pick you up at 7:40?"

"Of course. I'll be ready then. Is it casual or dressy?"

"It's dressy, I think, but not formal."

I mentally reviewed the few dresses I'd brought and decided a simple shift should work. It was the same emerald green as the pajamas Mom had packed. I had a black short-sleeved shrug I could throw over it to cover the nonexistent sleeves. "You can pick me up in the lobby of the BYU Women's Dormitory."

"The one on campus?"

"Yeah. There's only one. Most of the dorms were removed a couple of years ago to make room for other buildings and the underground parking. Off-campus housing is the norm now, but my parents felt more comfortable having me here."

"Oh. Well. I'll meet you there at 7:40 tomorrow night then."

"Sounds great." I hung up the phone and saw Nan's curious eyes on me.

"Are you going out?" She asked.

"Yes. I have a date tomorrow night to a dance at UVU."

"I didn't know you knew anyone there."

I smiled ruefully. "I don't."

Confusion flashed across her face. "Then who are you going with?"

"Henry rang up the sale on my bedding the other day."

"You're going out with a *stranger*?"

"I went out with your brother, didn't I?"

A deep furrow of concern rested between Nan's eyes. "That's different. Didn't he tell you I was his sister?"

I nodded. "He did, but I didn't really know you then…" My voice trailed off. The excuse was sounding weak, and we both heard it. I continued, "We're just going to the dance. I don't think much can happen in a crowd like that."

"Is he even a member?"

I shrugged. *Why didn't I think to ask?* I chided myself.

Nan tilted her head to the side, every strand of her perfectly coiffed hair remaining obediently in place. "Just be careful, Christina. Todd would never forgive me if something happened to you."

I stared at her a moment. *Why would Todd even care?*

Chapter 3, Dates

F riday evening, I stepped out the front glass doors of the dormitory at precisely 7:40. I could see Henry's dimple as he smiled at me from the front of a dark blue sedan that had seen better days. He turned his attention to the curb, where he was maneuvering to park between two much newer cars. I watched with amazement as he performed the feat. Kansas no longer required parallel parking in its driving test, so I'd never bothered to master the skill. I was impressed.

As he stepped out of the car, I could see that his charcoal gray sports coat over black dress pants would match my green dress. His conservative tie pulled the ensemble together nicely.

His deep voice interrupted my appreciation of his attire. "Nothing like promptness in a date." He enthused. "Ready?"

I nodded and followed him to his sedan where he opened the door with a flourish. It could have been a long sleek limousine for all the care he was showing. He seated me carefully, flashing his dimple again. His dimple brought a returning smile from me. I couldn't resist its charm.

As we drove to the UVU campus, I asked, "So…are you from around here?"

He shook his head, glanced at me, then focused back on the road. "I was raised in Battle Mountain, Nevada."

My brows furrowed in question. "What's in Battle Mountain?"

"Gold mining."

My eyes widened. "Oh." I was familiar with the price of gold. Gold was the investment of choice after the stock market had tanked.

"It's just a small town. There are less than 5,000 residents, but there are enough members to have a ward."

Relief flooded me. *At least he's a member.* Tentatively, I asked, "So did you serve a mission?"

His dimple flashed again. "Yes. I served in the California San Bernardino Mission."

"What was it like there?"

"I spent about half my mission in Yucca Valley. It wasn't much different from Battle Mountain except for the amount of people." He paused to glance at me. "Yucca Valley has about 20,000 inside the city limits. The surrounding area is dotted with five-acre plots. It's really something to see miles and miles of homes squatting in the middle of huge grassless yards."

My brain tried to fit around his image. I couldn't do it. I guess it was something I'd have to experience myself. "Did you have much success?"

"I baptized twenty people while on my mission, but they were all member referrals. We just taught them. We didn't find them."

"Isn't that a more successful approach, anyway?"

He nodded. "It is." He maneuvered his sedan into another tight parking spot. My car was smaller than his, but I wouldn't have dared park in the spot he chose.

I reached for his proffered arm, and we both headed into the dance. The music was loud enough to discourage much talking, so I didn't feel like I knew Henry much better than I had before the date when he dropped me off at the dorm. Other than offering his arm and the brief touching during our dances, we hadn't even held hands.

Nan pounced on me when I walked in the door to our room. "How did the date go?"

"Fine."

"What did you do?"

"We just danced a little. It was too loud to talk much, but I did find out he's a returned missionary."

"Well," she grimaced, "that's an improvement, anyway."

"Improvement on what?"

"On not knowing a thing about him."

"I have to agree with you there."

"Do you make a habit of going out with strangers?"

"Honestly," I couldn't hide the exasperation in my tone. "I haven't gone on many dates at all. It's hard to make a habit of anything if you've never done it."

Nan apologized. "I'm sorry. I'm just concerned, that's all."

"I'm sorry for sounding snippy." I said. "It's not like me. This dating thing is all new. We'll both adjust, I'm sure." Adjust to what was the golden question. I tried to scan Nan's face for answers, but she'd turned once again to her writing. For the first time, I was genuinely curious about what it was she was so furiously writing about.

Sunday evening Nan and I met Todd in front of the dorms. A warm summer breeze played with my long dark curls but left Nan's short cut in its forever-immaculate state. *What kind of hair care product creates such perfection?* I couldn't help the stray thought as we headed to the Marriott Center.

We strolled along casually, discussing weather and sports but carefully avoiding the hot topic of politics.

There were always politics with Israel. I'd never paid much attention to international matters, but with my two friends walking beside me, I couldn't help but wonder. *What would it feel like to live in a military zone?* Images of my childhood home in Salina flooded my mind. *The thought of a suicide bomber destroying my neighborhood never even entered my head.*

Uncomfortable with my thoughts, I tried to listen to the light chatter of the Cohens. *They seem happy enough. Maybe when you live in a war zone, you don't realize what you're missing by living in a peaceful community.* My brain simply couldn't envision a life of constant fear. A life where every citizen was required to spend some time in military service.

I peeked up at Todd and tried to see him in a military uniform. *I can't imagine him carrying a gun. Missionary badge and scriptures...yeah, I can see that. Gun? No way.*

When we reached the cement stairs that lead to the seating, Todd searched a moment then lead Nan and I to seating that didn't require moving down many steps. I smiled my appreciation. *It's so sweet of him to think about our heels.* While we waited for the room to fill, my mind wandered to Todd. *I wish I had a big brother to look after me. Nan is so lucky. It's obvious he adores her.*

A wave of homesickness washed over me. *I hope my little brothers and sisters know how much I adore them.* Thoughts of my siblings filled my head. They all had hair just slightly darker than Dad's—dishwater blond is what I'd heard it called. Tobias was the only one with Mom's hazel eyes. Everyone else inherited Dad's blue eyes. *Except me. But then, Dad isn't my birth father.* I shuddered as the dark thought engulfed me. My birth father wasn't someone I wanted to think about.

Nan reached into her purse and pulled out a clean handkerchief. "Are you okay, Christina?"

I nodded and took it with a shaky smile. "Just thinking about home." I dabbed at the tears and thought, *trust Nan to have an extra. I've never met someone so prepared in my life. She probably has a pack of bandages and a tiny screwdriver for glasses in there, too.* Thoughts of what Nan carried in her huge handbag had my tears dry and me stifling a snicker.

When the prophet walked in the room, the entire crowd stood up in unison and sang "We Thank Thee, Oh God, for a Prophet." He turned and smiled at the crowd. When he turned in my direction, I could feel his piercing stare look right into me, as if he could see into my heart. A true prophet of the living God was standing in my presence. I could feel the power of his link to the Divine in that one glance. I was grateful for the handkerchief as I pulled it out to wipe more tears. My homesickness was swept away in that one moment. *There is no other university that would give me an opportunity to be in the same room with a prophet of God.*

When he sat down, the congregation sat as well. I couldn't see any other dry eyes around me. There was power in the room, and it came from a source outside ourselves.

We were quiet as we walked back to the dorms, as if none of us wanted to break the spell. Todd offered a quiet farewell and kissed his sister's forehead. "See you tomorrow, Nan."

"Lunch?"

"Like always."

Then he was gone, his cologne lingering in the soft summer air. I stared after his parting back, a lump in my throat. His tender scene with Nan brought back all my homesickness in one fell swoop.

Chapter 4, Mark

Mom," I was sure my excitement carried over the phone lines, "I met the most amazing guy in my Physics class today."

"Oh," Mom's voice was careful, cautious. "What's he like?"

"Well, he returned from his mission in Peru about a year and a half ago."

Mom's relieved sigh could be heard over the phone.

I stifled a laugh. I knew what my mom wanted to hear, and it wasn't how good-looking he was. Since I got the important part over, I could fill in the details. "He's about Dad's height—a little over six feet, has short dark hair—about the same color as mine, and has gooorgeous gray eyes." I couldn't help drawing out the word. His eyes were divine.

"What's his family like?"

"Mo-om," my impatience sounded as clearly as my earlier excitement. "I just met the guy today. Give me some time."

"Okay." Mom paused for a split second. "What's his major?"

"He's in pre-law and will be graduating in the spring."

"Has he been accepted into law school?"

"He said he's been accepted by Stanford and Yale." This time, I was a little more hesitant. *Can someone be accepted without having graduated first? I don't even know how that works.*

Mom didn't seem to share my misgivings. "Those are some prestigious schools. I'm impressed."

"Believe me, he looks the part." I paused, trying to decide what I would tell her. "He's taking me to a fireside on Sunday. We'll be going to his sister's house afterwards for some dessert."

"That sounds like fun."

"It should be."

"How do you like your job?" Mom had bigger concerns than my love life. It wasn't too long ago that she'd heard me extol the virtues of Henry and Todd.

"I'm just the assistant to the secretary in the health sciences department. I mostly run errands and make copies."

"It's paying your living expenses, anyway."

"Yes. I'm grateful for that, and grateful that you and Dad are paying my housing and books. The scholarship doesn't go far." I walked to my desk and sat down, pulling the music theory text out of the neatly-ordered stack of books on my desk.

"We're glad we can help, and we're delighted that you chose to attend BYU."

"When Dad walked me around campus, he said it hadn't changed much from when he attended." I glanced at the syllabus and opened to the correct page while Mom answered.

"I wouldn't know. I went to UVU. I met Dad after he graduated."

I sighed. "I know. I know. I've heard the story before. Besides," I laughed, "I was there when you met, remember?"

Mom apologized. "I'm sorry. My old age is kicking in."

"Where you repeat the same stories over and over again?"

I could hear the smile in Mom's voice. "Something like that." Her voice grew serious. "How are your classes?"

"Economics is easy. So is the Book of Mormon class. My music appreciation class is hard." The words on music theory sitting on the page in front of me went blurry. Staying focused was a challenge, even when I wasn't sidetracked by a conversation with my mom.

"Why is that?"

"I have to memorize all kinds of music, know the composer and the year it was written." I groaned. "I've never had a musical ear, Mom. I'm scared I won't pass the class."

"Isn't there a CD that goes with the class?"

I sighed. "Yeah."

"Maybe you can just play the CD at night before you go to bed."

"I don't think that will help, Mom. How will I ever associate the composer with the music if I just listen at night?"

"Well, once you're familiar with the music, it will be easier to think of ways to remember who the composer is. Listen to the differences in musical instruments, tempos, that kind of thing."

I giggled. "You sound just like my professor." I lost my lighthearted tone. "I guess it's worth a try. The class is a real stretch for me."

"How is the Spanish class?"

"Um...it's a lot harder than my high school Spanish. We're required to speak in conversations. '¿Como se llama?' isn't much of a conversation."

Mom laughed sympathetically. "Yes. 'What do you call yourself?' is usually only used the first time you meet someone." She paused a moment, then continued, "Is there some tutoring available?"

"The professor mentioned some hours when tutors are available, but they're the same time as my work."

"What was the name of that guy you met?"

"Mark. Mark Sandstrom."

"Maybe Mark would be willing to help out."

"Do they speak Spanish in Peru?"

"I know there are groups that speak only the native Indian tongue, but I think Spanish is the national language."

I was doubtful. "I'll check with Mark and see what he says."

"You do that." Suddenly, Mom sounded distracted. She directed her next remark away from the phone. "Tobias, take that dog outside right now." Her attention back on me, she apologized. "I'm sorry, Christina. Peppy is covered in mud and Tobias brought him in. I'll talk to you later. I love you. Keep in touch."

I stifled a groan. *I don't want you to go.* "I love you, too, Mom. Hug everyone for me, please."

"I will. 'Bye."

I closed the cell phone and leaned back in the office chair facing the small desk that occupied the corner of my dorm room. A snapshot attached to the bulletin board with a white thumbtack stared back at me. It was a picture of my family standing in front of our home in Salina, Kansas. Even though I'd been in Provo for a few weeks, it seemed like a century. I hadn't realized how much I'd miss the family.

A small chuckle escaped as I envisioned the mess Peppy had made all over the kitchen floor. The white tile was easy to clean, but I was sure Tobias was getting a turn at learning how to mop the floor. He was my youngest brother. I could almost see his sandy-blond mop of hair glinting in the sun-lit kitchen as his six-year old hands were trying to mop up after the big Dane.

Discouraged at the swimming images on the textbook page, I shoved the syllabus inside the textbook to hold my place. I needed a few minutes to clear my head before I tried to tackle music theory.

I opened my laptop and checked my email. To my surprise, I had several notices from Facebook and Twitter. Some old friends had found me and had sent friend requests. I switched over to Facebook to accept the requests.

It was easy to get sidetracked by all the notices on my friend's walls. Before I knew it, an hour of my time had been eaten up. I sighed. This wasn't going to help me focus on my studies.

I switched over to Twitter and responded to a few Tweets. The shorthand was confusing, and there were a number of terms with the number sign attached to the front. I clicked on a few and soon figured out they must be the "hash tags" my friends would talk about. If I wanted to read more on a subject preceded by a number sign, I just clicked on the link and could read whatever was tweeted about it.

Watching real-time conversations between people who might never meet each other in real life was eerie. Like watching a giant multiplayer game in action where the game had no end and the people involved didn't know how to quit.

I glanced over my few followers. Since I'd picked a Japanese handle, I wasn't surprised to find a handful of Japanese followers. I snickered. There was no way I could read any of their posts. I'd have to get my dad's brother-in-law, Brett, or Todd to read them. In the meantime, I had work to do. I decisively logged out and turned back to my dreaded music theory textbook.

Three days later, I checked the black alarm clock sitting on the small dresser next to my bed. Mark would be picking me up in ten minutes.

I looked in the mirror hanging on the back of the bedroom door and smoothed my hair. A strand had chosen to break free from the hairspray I'd applied just a few moments before. My friends had always envied my curls. I wished my hair would stay as flat as I tried to keep it with a straightener. There were always a few strands that refused to comply.

My makeup was flawless. At least something was going right.

I was glad Nan was out spending some time with her brother. She would have been amused. I had changed outfits three times. I inspected the navy knee-length skirt and matching blazer. A couple of stray white hairs, probably from Peppy, clung to the wool. A quick brush with a pet roller cleared the hair. The ensemble was finished with a white collared shirt, the creases crisp and fresh.

I wasn't sure how I should dress for a fireside at BYU with Mark. I hadn't worried so much about impressing Todd and Henry, but I knew Mark was planning to be a lawyer. Even in this modern day, I suspected he'd want his date to seem like an equal. He didn't intimidate me, exactly, but I wanted him to feel like I was a worthy companion.

I glanced at the clock again. Five more minutes. I might as well head down to the lobby. Men weren't allowed in the girls' bedrooms. The honor code at BYU was as unchangeable as the bedrock under "Y" mountain.

When I stepped into the lobby, Mark hadn't arrived, so I settled into one of the leather chairs next to a flower arrangement. The scent of fresh flowers should have been relaxing, but my heart raced. I glanced nervously around the room and smiled at a few of the other girls I'd met in the cafeteria. They were waiting for their dates, too.

I sat at the edge of my seat. *Think prim and proper.* I crossed my ankles and hoped I looked presentable. *Why am I so worried? It's just a walk to the Marriott Center and then dessert at his sister's. He's just a guy. Get over it.*

After several young men had arrived and then left with their dates, I snuck a glance at the lobby clock. Mark was two minutes late. *It's not like I've been on a lot of dates yet. The Salina Ward just didn't have any guys available.* I took a deep breath to calm my nerves and smiled brightly as the door opened once more.

It was Mark. He looked perfect—not a hair out of place, and his charcoal gray pinstriped suit would compliment my navy blue one. *Phew. At least I made the right wardrobe choice.*

His gray eyes scanned the room then warmed when he saw me. I stood up as he strode across the room. "Christina, I thought you'd forgotten."

"Not a chance," I smiled up at him as he offered me his arm. He was at least a foot taller than I was. I put my hand lightly in the crook of his arm, and we headed out the door. The combined scent of citrus and musk floated up from Mark's jacket. It reminded me of gardens and summer. The scent was calming. As I breathed it in, my heartbeats slowed. *All that stress for nothing. He's just a guy.*

The Marriott Center was only a few minutes away. Despite my silent pep-talk and my slower heart rate, I still felt intimidated. I tried to scan my brain for something to say. *Why did this gorgeous guy choose me? Surely he could have his pick of girls on campus.*

I glanced up at him. He seemed intent on leading us safely to the fireside. The grim set of his jaw made me

41

hesitant. *What if I say something really stupid? I'm awfully good at it.* I bit my lip and tried to keep up with his long strides. I had to take two steps for every one of his. By the time we reached the Marriott Center, I was so out of breath, I couldn't carry on a decent conversation.

As the crowd forced us to slow, Mark glanced down at me, a worried crease between his brows. "I'm sorry. Was I walking too fast for you?"

I tried to hide a wry smile. "I was feeling like we were in a marathon for a few minutes there, but I think I'll be alright. My years in track helped."

His surprised expression looked comical. "You were in track?"

"Yeah. I spent four years running marathons, but I didn't break any records."

Just then, Mark found an opening in the crowd and pulled me behind him into the arena. We wound our way down the stairs and settled into the middle of a section.

I didn't like stairs—especially while wearing heels. I'd fallen down our main staircase more than once growing up. Of course, a few of those times had been when I was attempting to ride the banister to the main floor. Mom had rules about that. She had rules about everything. I bit my lip to hide a smile at the thought. I didn't want Mark wondering what I was thinking about. *I doubt he wants to know all about Mom and her rules.*

As he helped me move into the aisle he'd chosen, Mark whispered, "You're trembling." Mark's gray eyes looked down into mine with surprise. "What's the matter?"

"I just don't like mixing stairs and heels, that's all."

When we were both seated, he put his arm around my waist. "I can tell." He grinned. "Nice excuse for holding you close."

I wrinkled my nose at him. "As if you needed one."

He chuckled then turned his attention to the words to the opening hymn flashing across the screen above the crowd. He started to sing, and I joined in. The hymn helped me relax. I forgot about the stairs until the fireside was over.

When Mark started to rise, I touched his arm to restrain him. "Can we please wait until the crowd thins out a little?"

He looked irritated. "I promised Jeanette we'd be at her place by 8:30."

Why is he so angry? He seemed compassionate earlier. "I'm sure it won't take long to clear out." I paused and looked up at him with pleading eyes. "I'd really like to wait a bit."

He settled back. "Oh. All right. If you insist." He tapped his foot and looked at his watch.

What's the hurry? I thought. *Surely he can wait a few minutes.* I could feel my anger rise.

As the crowd streamed by, Mark stood up again then looked down at me. "Is this good enough for you?"

Anxious to keep him happy and stifling my anger, I nodded and swallowed. I didn't want to fight the crowds and the stairs at the same time, but there weren't nearly as many people moving from our section. *Quit being a baby.* I chided myself. *You can do this.*

I managed to work my way up the stairs behind Mark without tripping. I missed his comforting hand. *Why isn't he helping me like he did before? Did I do something wrong?* I puzzled over the problem as I worked my way up the steps. *I can't remember even saying anything.* I sighed with relief when we reached the main floor.

Mark reached for my hand. "See. It wasn't so bad, was it?"

I shook my head, out of breath and not sure what I would say. *Was he trying to teach me a lesson? He doesn't seem as aware of my feelings as Dad is of Mom's, but maybe age mellows guys out. Dad is years older than Mark. I can't imagine that Mark really doesn't care about how I feel. He's just immature. That's it. He needs a little time to grow up.* I snuck another look at him through my lashes. *He's a returned missionary. He's excelling in his studies. He's a worthy priesthood holder. He's an amazing guy and oh, so…gorgeous. Who am I to criticize? It's not like I'm Miss Perfect.*

We walked up the hill to his car. I was even more out of breath during this walk than I was for the first one. An uphill jog was hard even when I was training daily for marathons. I was out of shape with the summer off and just a month into the fall semester at BYU.

As Mark pulled me to a stop next to a light gray Camaro Coupe, I wasn't surprised by his choice of car. Not a family car. *It's his commuting car.* I reasoned then stifled a laugh. *Hybrid or not, I seriously doubt it gets good gas mileage.* "Nice car." *I hope my voice hides my disapproval.*

"It was a gift from my parents. They gave it to me after I returned home from my mission." Mark's voice almost purred with pride as he opened the passenger door for me. As I stepped in, new car smell enveloped me. I relaxed against the gray leather seats and breathed in the smell. *He returned from his mission almost a year and a half ago. How can it still smell new?*

The scent reminded me of the time Dad had taken me to test drive cars. In the end, we picked a used car. It was the hunter green economy car that spent most of its time parked in the parking garage under the dormitories.

Mark pressed a button on his key chain that closed my door and then one that opened his. His door closed when he inserted the key. The headlights and taillights went on at the same time. A mechanical female voice asked, "Destination?"

Mark answered the computer. "Jeanette Nielsen."

"Jeanette Nielsen. Destination Confirmed."

A screen on the dashboard flashed a map of the Provo/Orem area. The words "Jeanette Nielsen" flashed inside a red beacon before the screen went dark.

The engine came to life. The quiet electric engine was enhanced by the required amount of noise. I remembered when the legislation had gone through for the sound enhancers. They were a federal requirement demanded by Advocates for the Blind.

Every elementary student knew hybrid cars used both gas and electricity. When the battery was low, the gas engine roared to life. The electric engine didn't emit the same sound. It required sound amplifiers so the blind wouldn't step into traffic when an electric car approached.

Mark sat back in his seat and casually watched the cars heading in the opposite direction. His request for his sister's house had put the car on autopilot. He wouldn't need to do anything until the car parked in front of her house.

My car was one of the old-fashioned kind that required manual steering. Mom and Dad thought I should know how to drive a "real car" just in case the computer shut down for some reason. They were scared if I relied on autopilot too much, I'd panic if it ever died. Their fear for me is what persuaded them to get me a used car. I shuddered. I'd seen a few accidents in my life. They were all the persuasion I needed.

We pulled into a long, curved driveway in front of a large three-story house. The cream-colored stucco walls were obviously new—nothing like the century-old slate gray walls of my home in Salina. Lighted windows welcomed us, and I could see a few young faces pressed against an upstairs window. *Mark's nieces and nephews must be curious about me.*

The car pulled to a stop behind a deep blue SUV. *Perfect for a big family*, I thought.

The Camaro's doors opened, and the engine shut off. *What am I supposed to do? The door is already open. Do I wait for Mark or just step out?*

After a moment's hesitation, I joined him as he stepped to the curb. He pushed a button, and both doors shut. A slight click after the doors closed assured me they were locked.

Large solid wooden front doors flew open as we walked up the few broad steps to the house. I thought I recognized a couple of faces that had just peered at us through a second story window. *They must've sprinted down the stairs.* I stared past them into the house then hid a grin. *Or slid down the banister. I'll bet their Mom wasn't thrilled.*

A short plumpish woman, her face slightly pink from embarrassment or the after effects of anger at her children, I couldn't tell, hurried to the door. She brushed a long mahogany strand of hair out of her green eyes. She sounded breathless as she greeted me. "Hi. I'm Jeanette. You must be Christina." She held her hand out for a friendly handshake. "Mark told us all about you."

My own cheeks burned as I stretched out my hand. *I wonder what he said about me. He hadn't introduced himself to me until earlier this week.* I peeked up at him.

He had the grace to look embarrassed, as well. "Don't believe everything Jeanette says. She has a tendency to exaggerate."

Jeanette released her grip on my hand then stamped her small foot on the tiled entryway. The tile matched the color of the stucco on the outside walls of the home. "You've been talking about Christina since the first day of class." Her twinkling smile and quick wink at me belied the angry stomp.

My eyes widened in surprise. *I had no idea he's been interested since class started. That was almost four weeks ago. What's the fascination? I'm not nearly as pretty as most of the other girls in class.* I studied Mark's flushed face a moment, then followed Jeanette to the large dining room to the right of the staircase. The table was as big as the one in my own home in Salina. Four boisterous boys and a couple of girls had rushed in ahead of us.

A large blond man sat at the table. His blue eyes crinkled in a welcome smile as he stood up and stretched out his hand to envelope mine in a firm handshake. "Hi. I'm Stanley Nielsen. You can call me Stan. I'm Jeanette's husband and these ruffians' dad."

The youngest looked up, startled. "What's a ruffian?"

Stan released my hand then reached down to ruffle the boy's mahogany hair. The color was a perfect match to Jeanette's. "A little devil like you." The affection in his voice softened the statement. Stan looked up at me then. "This is Daniel. He's five."

Stan glanced around the table at his other children. "Krystal is the blond sitting next to him. She's seven. David, the other blond, is eight. Kallia is ten. Dennis was ordained a deacon last week."

Stan paused while I reached out to shake Dennis's hand. His hair was a warm brown, not quite as red as his mother's. It matched Kallia's hair. "Congratulations. That's really cool."

Jeanette beamed with pride and continued the introductions. "Dean is a Teacher and Darrill is a Priest."

"I'll bet they keep you busy."

"Yes. The older the kids get, the more time they seem to need. I always thought it would get easier when they got older, but it hasn't turned out that way."

"I'm sure." I sympathized as best as I could, but I was still on the receiving end of a mother's time. It would be a while before I'd really know what she was talking about.

Mark pulled out a chair for me about halfway down the table. He sat next to me while trying to fend off the punches of his sixteen-year-old nephew, Darrill. Darrill's blond hair was almost white. *The same color as Henry's.* I mused. *I wonder what Henry is up to?* Kallia's giggle as Mark was fending off Darrill's punches brought me back to the moment.

All of the kids shared their dad's blue eyes. I peered up at Mark. *Will his kids have his beautiful gray eyes?* I stopped myself. *Not if I'm their mom.* I stifled a sigh. *My children will all have brown eyes. No use wishing for something I can't have.*

Jeanette had left and then entered with a large bucket of vanilla ice cream. Kallia and Krystal followed behind with bananas and toppings. Stan carried in bowls and spoons.

"It's a 'make-it-yourself night,' so dig in." Jeanette smiled as she settled the bucket in the middle of the table.

I relaxed at the banter around the table. The sounds reminded me of my home in Salina. It was impossible not to feel comfortable.

After we finished our banana splits, I looked at Jeanette. "Do you need help with the dishes?"

She shook her head emphatically. "No. It's the boys' turn for dishes tonight." She stopped and glared at them. "They can handle it just fine."

At her stern look, the older boys jumped up to gather the dishes and walk them into the kitchen. Jeanette raised her eyebrows at Daniel. "Don't you need to be doing something?"

"I'm too little to help."

"I don't think so." Jeanette's voice was firm.

Stan joined in. "Go help your brothers. You know how to load the dishwasher. They can rinse and you can load."

"Okay, Daddy." Daniel hopped off his chair and moved to the kitchen.

I hid a smile. I was sure a similar scene was playing out at my own home.

Mark spoke up. "Since you don't need our help, I'll take Christina back to her dorm. Physics starts early."

Jeanette was curious, and she directed her question at me. "How come you're taking Physics? What's your major?"

I shrugged. "I wanted to get my science courses out of the way. I haven't decided on a major yet."

Jeanette nodded. "It can be a tough decision." She laughed at herself. "I changed majors four times."

It was my turn to be curious. "What did you end up majoring in?"

"Child psychology." Jeanette grinned. "I just didn't know you had to re-learn everything with each kid."

I smiled sympathetically. "My mom says every one of us has been so different, it was like trying to learn a whole new language."

"How many kids are in your family?" Mark wanted to know.

"I have three brothers and two sisters."

"How old are they?" Jeanette asked.

"Mary is 12, Nathan is 11, Coby is 9, Julie is 8, and Tobias is 6."

Jeanette stared at me with her green eyes. I could almost watch the calculator in her brain at work. "Wow. There's quite a gap between you and Mary, isn't there?"

I nodded then bit my lip and glanced at Mark. *I wasn't going to mention where I fit in the family just yet, but I don't know why I'm uncomfortable sharing. It isn't like I did anything wrong.* "Garrett adopted me when he and my mother married."

"Oh? Were your parents divorced?" Jeanette asked.

My eyes went wide. *She sure is nosy.*

Sensing my discomfort, Stan broke in. "I'm sure Mark and Christina need to get home." He stood up to usher us out. I sent him a small smile of gratitude. Jeanette's face went a rosy pink. *At least she has the grace to be embarrassed.*

Mark and I were quiet as we loaded into the car.

"Destination?" the car's computer asked.

"Christina Andrews."

"Christina Andrews. Destination confirmed."

Once again, the computer screen flashed the Provo/Orem area. This time, the red beacon read "Christina Andrews."

How many other girls' apartments are programmed into his car? I wondered.

I stared out the window as the car headed to the dorms and was startled when Mark asked, "So…what happened to your dad?"

"He died."

"Oh."

I shuddered, and Mark put his warm hand over mine. That time, the citrus and musk blend rising from his suit coat did nothing to relax me. I met his eyes then turned to the window. *I don't feel like telling him about my rapist father. The man who wanted to kill my mother and died while he was chasing us.* The flood of memories during that awful night brought tears to my eyes. It was a memory I wished I didn't have.

"I'm sorry." Mark's voice was meant to be comforting.

I fought back tears. *How can he comfort me when he has no idea what I've been through?*

We were both quiet the rest of the trip, lost in our own thoughts.

When the Camaro pulled up in front of the dorms, Mark pressed a button to open the door. I stepped out.

"I'll see you" I couldn't prevent the catch in my voice, "in Physics tomorrow?" *Will he want to see me again?*

"Yeah." He smiled. "I need the credits for graduation. I'll be there."

I watched as his car moved down the street, then turned and walked into the women's dormitory.

I wasn't looking forward to heading to bed. This was going to be a nightmare night. I could feel it. Scenes from the night my birth father died flashed through my mind.

Chapter 5, Los Hermanos

When I walked through the door of the Physics class the next morning, Mark looked relaxed and invigorated. I felt like death warmed over. My night had been just as full of nightmares as I'd anticipated.

Hesitant, I moved to the chair next to him. When he smiled up at me, I thought, *I must not look as awful as I feel.* I smiled back and took the seat.

"Did you sleep well?" Mark asked.

I nodded. *I don't want him knowing how freaked out I am about what happened.* I stared ahead at the professor. *He'd think I'm a basket case.*

Mark was close enough I could smell the cologne he'd put on that morning. It was distinctly different from whatever he'd been wearing the night before. It was clean, crisp, invigorating, and impossible to ignore.

About halfway through the lecture, Mark pressed his leg next to mine. My eyes opened wide. This was something I wasn't prepared for. *If I move away, he'll think I don't like him, but I don't like his leg next to mine. It's too soon in the relationship for this.* I spent the rest of the class trying to ignore his leg pressing against mine. It was hard to concentrate on the lecture when my whole body was aware of his. And his *scent.* Wow.

As the professor ended her lecture and I gathered up my notes, Mark leaned over and moved my long brown hair away from my ear. His breath tickled my neck as he whispered, "I was wondering what you're doing for lunch."

A shiver ran down my back. His intimacy was disconcerting. I turned to him and opened my eyes wide in surprise. *Two dates in a row? Am I supposed to do that? Well, Dad said I didn't need to worry about dating a variety of guys in college. The 'no steady dating rule' was just for high school.* I bit my lip on a smile. *Not like I had any chance at steady dating before.*

Since the professor was finished with her lecture, I didn't feel the need to whisper back, but my tone wasn't loud enough to carry far. "I was just planning to eat at the cafeteria." I stared at him a moment, then asked, "Why? Did you have something in mind?"

"Something off campus, maybe?"

"I can't go far. I need to study and then I work at 1:00 at the Health Sciences Department."

Mark's brow furrowed. "What do you do there?"

"I'm an assistant secretary in the Dean's office."

"Something after work, then? What time do you get off?"

"I work until 5:00."

"Do you like Mexican food?"

I nodded and smiled. "Love it."

"Great. There's a really good Mexican restaurant on the corner of University and Main. Los Hermanos."

"I've heard good things about it, but I've never eaten there." I said.

"Consider it a date, then." He paused and reached for my hand as I stood up and slung the backpack over my shoulder. "Where to now?"

"I'm heading to Spanish." I pulled my hand away from his. He looked down at me, startled. "I meant to ask you…Do you speak Spanish?"

He nodded. "Peru was a Spanish-speaking mission."

"I was wondering," I paused again and searched his face, unsure of his response, "if you could help tutor me in Spanish. It's a lot harder than I anticipated."

He smiled and nodded. "I'd love to. When did you want to start?"

"I have some time right after my Spanish class. Can you spare an hour then?"

"Of course. I'll meet you after class." Mark reached for my hand again. This time, I didn't pull away as he led me out of the room and on to my next class.

I was concentrating on typing out notes for one of the dean's books when I was startled by a tap on my shoulder. Mark laughed at my slight jump. "It's 5:00." His breath tickled my ear. "Did I scare you?"

I pulled back to look at him and wrinkled my nose. "I forgot you were coming. Let me shut down the computer, and I need to leave a note for Leslie so she can know where I left off." I handled the two tasks while Mark looked over my shoulder. *Yikes. Personal space is something he must not need.*

I grabbed my backpack, scanned the room to make sure I hadn't forgotten anything, then shut off the lights as we headed out of the room. "Leslie is attending a board meeting right now. She asked me to lock up." I double-checked the door to make sure the lock had latched. Mark reached for my hand. It felt warm and secure, not clammy like Henry's hand. Henry had finally held my hand the previous Friday when we'd gone to a movie. *Mark's changed scents again.* I thought with surprise. *Does this guy have a scent for every clothing change?*

My cell phone rang as we headed down the hall. I glanced at the number. It was Todd. Not wanting to bother

Mark with my personal life, I rejected the call then turned the phone off.

Mark asked, "Anything serious?"

"No. It was just a friend. I'll call him back later."

"Oh. Okay." His eyes were flinty. "Do you have many friends?"

I laughed. "A few. Most of my friends from Kansas are attending BYU." *No need to tell him I've made more friends here in the first few weeks in Provo than I have my entire life.* "It's the gathering place for young adult members from all over the world."

He chuckled. "You sound like a brochure. BYU—the place to be."

"Advertiser extraordinaire. That's me." I giggled then reached for his hand.

Just as it had the previous night, his long gait had me breathless by the time we reached his car. Apparently, in-transit time to any destination wouldn't be used for talking. Meandering wasn't in his vocabulary.

As we took our seats in the car, the computer's voice asked, "Destination?"

"Manual override."

"Manual override confirmed. Autopilot off."

Seeming to sense my curiosity, Mark said, "Parking is difficult to find next to Los Hermanos. I want the freedom to wait for a parking spot if I have to."

Since my own car didn't have autopilot, I had no idea how the car parking would work.

"If I left it up to the computer, we'd probably be parked three blocks away."

I nodded, pretending to understand what he was talking about.

As we turned right on the street in front of the restaurant, I could see what Mark meant. *Los Hermanos must be popular,* I mused. All the parking stalls down the street were full.

Todd had called a couple of weeks before to take me to Los Hermanos, but Henry had already invited me to a movie so I had to postpone the date. *I'm guessing Todd's call was him trying to set another time for our dinner. He sure is being persistent for a big-brother type,* I thought.

Mark made a U-turn at the end of the block and slowly headed back up the street. Just as he'd anticipated, a car's backing lights came on a couple of stalls ahead. Mark stopped and waited for the owner of the car to vacate the spot. The Camaro pulled in smoothly behind the departing car. "Perfect." Mark grinned. "Let's go eat."

I stepped out of the car as the automatic doors opened then moved to the curb of the parking strip to wait for Mark. He reached for my hand. When I trembled at his touch, Mark responded with a temporary tightening of his fingers.

He dropped my hand so he could open the heavy glass doors of the restaurant. Spices perfumed the air.

Before I had a chance to decipher the scents, the maitre d' greeted us. Her nametag read "Clara." "Table for two?" she asked brightly.

Mark nodded.

"There's a 15-minute wait."

Mark interrupted. "I have reservations. Sandstrom. 5:20."

Clara scanned her list, her brow furrowed, then smoothed when she found his reservation. "Here it is. Come this way."

We followed her brisk pace around large potted plants and to the side of the restaurant facing University Avenue. The outside walls were shaped like a large greenhouse. The top windows slanted down to join the straight side windows. I wasn't sure I wanted every pedestrian walking down University to watch me eat, so I was relieved when Clara led us to a secluded table next to a solid brick wall that had once been the outside of the restaurant. A large planter next to the table housed a tall fern. Its branches acted as a natural screen. I didn't know how much extra Mark had to pay for the privacy, but it was worth every penny.

While Mark helped to seat me, Clara placed two large menus on the table. "Dan will be your server tonight. He'll be here shortly."

Mark nodded as he sat at the other side of the table. "Thanks."

I picked up the menu and scanned the variety of authentic Mexican dishes. I decided my tastes ran to more familiar Americanized food.

"Did you want an appetizer?" Mark interrupted my concentration.

I met his gaze and wondered what to say without making a fool of myself. *I'd like some chips and salsa, but those are normally free at a Mexican restaurant. Am I supposed to mention chips and salsa as an appetizer? Would asking for them make me look like a redneck?* Seconds ticked by.

"Well?" Mark's voice started to sound impatient.

I drew in a breath then tried to blow it out without him seeing I needed to calm myself. "Chips and salsa would be nice."

"Hot salsa or mild?"

"Is there a choice?"

Mark stared at me like I'd grown an extra head.

I could feel a blush warming my cheeks.

"I forgot you haven't been here before." Mark dropped his gaze and pointed at the menu, where it was clearly displayed. "Hot and mild are available. You can try both, if you want."

"I'd like that."

Our server's arrival was just in time. I needed a moment to get composed. "Hi. I'm Dan. I'll be your server tonight. Can I interest you in one of our specialty drinks?"

I glanced at Mark. *I doubt money's an object.* I looked up at Dan. "What do you recommend?"

"The virgin Piña Colada is very good."

"What's that?" I asked.

"It's like a coconut pineapple smoothie." Dan informed me then continued. "The virgin strawberry daiquiri is very good, too."

"I think I'll try the virgin Piña Colada."

Dan nodded and turned to Mark, who said, "I'll have the alcohol-free Piña Colada as well."

My brows furrowed for a moment. *Did I call my drink the wrong thing? Maybe using the word 'virgin' bothered him. Not that it had any meaning other than alcohol-free in this context. Sheesh. Here I go, putting my foot in my mouth again.* My brow cleared. Mark hadn't seemed to notice my fleeting change of expression.

Dan was asking, "Did you want an appetizer to go with your drinks?"

Since we'd already discussed appetizers, Mark didn't wait for my response. "We'd like both versions of the house salsa delivered with the chips."

Dan nodded and disappeared. He was back with the drinks and chips so quickly I hadn't had time to think of anything to say to Mark.

I unwrapped the straw Dan had delivered with the drink. Not sure what to do with the slice of pineapple attached to the side of the glass, I left it right where it was. As I sipped out of the tall glass, my eyebrows rose in appreciation. The sweet icy blend of coconut and pineapple was an unexpected delight. "This is really good."

Mark nodded. "Los Hermanos has an outstanding reputation. I thought you'd like it."

I was glad for the icy drink after a bite of the spicy salsa. I almost choked on the chip.

Mark grinned. "I should've warned you. I think they just crush up jalapeño peppers and add a couple of tomatoes. It takes some time to adjust to the heat." He dipped his house-made white corn chip into the green salsa. He had a serving the size of a tablespoon on the chip. As he munched on the chip and salsa combination, I was surprised there weren't tears in his eyes. He might be mentally prepared for the heat, but his body would surely react in some way. I watched in astonishment as he continued to dip his chips into the spicy green salsa.

How can he do that? I could feel the steam coming out of my ears after just one *bite.* After another sip of my Piña Colada, I picked up a thin warm triangle. This time, I dipped the chip into the redder salsa. The salsa was mild enough for me to eat; and the blend of spices was a culinary delight. My eyes widened in surprise.

"I never thought I'd say this about salsa, but this is…" I struggled to find the words. Mark's presence always left me tongue tied and I couldn't think of anything that would adequately describe the unique blend of flavors combined in the deceptively simple bowl of salsa.

"Something else?"

I nodded.

Dan approached our table again. "Have you decided what you'd like to eat?" He directed his question to me.

"Yes. I'll have the taco salad with grilled chicken."

"Would you like ranch dressing with that?"

I nodded again and glanced at Mark. *Ranch seems safe. Surely there won't be any jalapeños in it.* My tongue still burned from the mouthful of green salsa I'd tried earlier.

"I'll have the steak fajitas." Mark said when Dan looked at him.

Dan scribbled into his notepad, collected the menus, then quietly disappeared.

My attention turned to Mark. He was rubbing my foot with his. I'd always thought that would be a turn on, but I was not feeling turned on. I was feeling annoyed. *How can I let him know I need my space without upsetting him?* Desperate for an excuse to pull my foot away, I nudged the purse I'd left on the floor with my opposite foot until the purse was almost touching Mark's foot, then I switched out my foot for the purse. I wondered how long it would take him to realize he wasn't touching my body. I bit my lip to prevent a giggle.

I didn't get a chance to see if Mark would notice or not. Mark sat up as Dan arrived with my salad and a round cast iron flat pan hot enough that the meat and sliced onions were sizzling on the platter.

He placed my salad in front of me, then turned to Mark and cautioned, "Careful. This is hot." Dan settled the hissing platter in front of Mark. He placed a plate of white flatbread next to the platter and finished with another plate of fresh chopped tomatoes, lettuce, guacamole, sour cream, and shredded cheese.

My eyes widened in surprise. "That's enough food to feed a small army."

Mark chuckled. "They do serve nice portions. How is the salad?"

"I don't know. I haven't tried it yet." I turned my attention to my own food. The ranch dressing was served in a small cup next to the taco shell bowl that held my salad. I poured the creamy white dressing over the chicken slices and spring lettuce mix. As I pushed the fork through the salad for a bite, I noticed the avocado and tomato slices. Small black olive slices added additional color, as did the grated cheddar cheese. I took a bite and nodded appreciatively. After I swallowed, I said, "This is really good. Thanks for bringing me here."

Mark smiled warmly. "My pleasure."

We spent the next few minutes enjoying our meal. When Mark finished, he pushed back his chair slightly. "Did you want dessert?"

I shook my head. "I'm stuffed." I stared down at the half-eaten salad with regret. *I'd ask for a box to take this home, but I don't know how Mark would feel about it.* "I can't eat another bite." I fiddled with the tablecloth.

"Did you want to go to a movie?"

I shook my head. "No. I need to study for my music test. We have a quiz every Tuesday."

His eyebrows lifted in surprise. "That's a lot of tests."

"Well, it works out better for me. I have a hard enough time remembering all the composers. Having them broken down into smaller units is very helpful. I just hope I can remember enough to pass the final at the end of the semester."

Mark reached out to touch my hand. "I'm sure you'll do fine."

He looked up as Dan approached with the tab. When Dan left, Mark tucked a couple of bills in with the receipt. As we were leaving, I looked back at Dan, who was picking up the folder with the money. His look of disgust revealed Mark's stingy tip. I was surprised. Mark's belongings certainly spoke of money, and he didn't act like money was an object.

What's the deal with that? Mark knows most the servers in town are students just like us. Students struggling to make ends meet. Why wouldn't he be generous with his tip? I glanced up at him then dropped my gaze. *I guess he's not perfect, after all. But then, neither am I.* With that final thought, I pushed Mark's faux pas out of my mind.

The drive back to my dorm was quiet. Mark wasn't much of a talker, and I couldn't ever think of anything witty or clever to say.

It was nearing the end of September. The air was crisp and clear. Still silent, we walked toward the gleaming glass doors. The evening wasn't yet dark, so I was surprised when Mark pulled me off to the side of the entrance to stand on the grass. He bent his head toward mine, and I could sense his desire for a kiss. I reached up and touched his lips. "Don't."

His brows furrowed. "Why? What's wrong?"

"I don't want to kiss anyone until over the altar of the temple, or at least until I'm engaged."

He chuckled. "Why? What does it matter? I've kissed tons of girls."

I fought to control a desire to roll my eyes. *Why does that NOT surprise me?* "It matters to me. I don't care how many girls you've kissed." *I really don't*, I thought. "But it matters to me. It's a goal I've had all my life."

"Don't let me be the one to break it." Mark sounded irritated.

I snickered. "Don't worry. I won't." I paused a moment and watched the anger fade from his face. "See you tomorrow?"

"Physics is a Monday, Wednesday, Friday class." He said.

"That's right. I forgot."

Mark gave me a measured look. "Would you like to see a movie tomorrow night?"

"I'm sorry. I can't. I try not to stay out late. With my job, I only have the evenings to study. I prefer to save my dating for weekends."

"You have to eat. Can I take you somewhere for dinner, then?"

I thought about Dan's angry expression. *Do I really want to go out with someone who won't even leave a decent tip?* Then I looked at Mark. His gray eyes and dark hair were the best looking combination I'd ever seen. And his athletic physique didn't hurt, either. *He's a returned missionary. That counts for something, too.*

"Well?" Mark's voice was growing impatient again.

"Ummm. Yeah. It beats the cafeteria, that's for sure, and I have to say, I enjoy the company." I sent him an impish smile.

"I'll pick you up at your office at 5:00 then." He turned on his heel and left, not waiting for a reply.

My mouth dropped open in surprise. I didn't remember to close it again until he and his Camaro were out of sight.

"Cute tongue." Todd's amused voice brought my head up and my tongue in.

"I didn't even know it was out." I could feel a blush warm my cheeks.

"That was obvious. You looked intent on your work. What are you typing?"

"It's a manuscript for one of the professors. Something about the link between celiac disease and the new fast-rising yeast."

Todd's eyebrows rose in surprise. "Sounds...interesting."

I glanced down at the manuscript. "It's certainly a unique thought, anyway. I would've never made the connection. I'm not sure what to think."

He changed the subject. "Do you have a moment to celebrate with us?"

Nan peeked around her brother. They were both wearing white. My brows wrinkled in confusion. "What kind of celebration?"

"It's Rash Hashanah. The Jewish New Year."

"Oh." *And this means what to me?* I stared up at them.

Nan sighed. "The Feast of Trumpets." I was so not getting it. "The day Joseph Smith received the golden plates."

I hit my forehead with the palm of my hand. "Duh. My Book of Mormon teacher was talking about it last week. There was a whole section devoted to it in *Days of Awe*. Sorry. My brain is on yeast right now."

Nan snickered. "The way your brain is functioning, you'd think it was full of it."

I giggled. "So... how do we celebrate Rash Hashanah?"

"With a sweet treat." Nan pulled out a small covered bowl and pulled off the lid. The golden liquid didn't move. *Honey?*

Todd pulled out another bowl. That one was full of sliced apples. *My favorite*, I thought. *But with honey? Yikes.*

I slid the huge vase of red roses out of the way. Todd raised his brows in a question but didn't ask. I didn't answer his unspoken question. I didn't want to explain about Mark. Besides, it was annoying that Mark would claim me like some kind of cow. I wasn't his to claim, and I didn't want Todd thinking I was taken.

Roseanne Evans Wilkins

Chapter 6, Anniversary

"I brought you something." Mark's voice interrupted my concentration. I looked up from the manuscript I was typing to smile at him.

"What is it this time?"

"One guess."

Since I could see a few buds poking out from behind his back, it wasn't hard to figure out. "Umm...flowers?"

"Right. But these are special."

I glanced over at the simple green vase of wilting red roses still sitting on my desk. They were the replacement bouquet for the flowers Mark had brought the Monday after our date to Los Hermanos. "Those ones weren't special?"

"They weren't anniversary flowers." Mark pulled out the flowers he'd been hiding behind his back and presented them with a flourish. "Ta dah."

My eyes widened. It was a dozen red roses in a crystal vase. A brilliant blue butterfly, its open delicate wings looking almost real, rested on a twig extending above the flowers. "Wow. I don't know what to say."

"Say you'll go out with me."

"I already did." I laughed up at him. "Where did you say we were going?"

"First, dinner at Los Hermanos."

"We haven't been there in four weeks. I'd like that."

"I thought you might." He paused and looked down at my uplifted face. "I know you have rules about nothing but dinner on weekdays, but since this is our first month anniversary, I'd like to do something special."

My brain quit working when he said "anniversary" that way. Like it was the start of many. *Week anniversary. Month anniversary. That implied there were going to be year anniversaries, didn't it?* I stared up at Mark with a glazed expression.

He sounded impatient. "Did you hear what I was saying?"

"Sorry," I apologized, "my mind was on something else." I bit my lip on a laugh as Mark's expression grew stormy.

"How can you think about something else when I'm talking about our anniversary date?"

"Calm down. Calm down," I snickered, "I was just thinking about the past month." I paused and tilted my head. "We've been eating out every weekday, we've watched a movie every Friday, watched some kind of sporting event on Saturday, and we've spent every Sunday evening at Jeanette's house. I've hardly had a moment to myself since our first date." For a moment, Nan's disapproving face blurred my vision. She hadn't been happy.

"Is that a bad thing?" Mark sounded hurt.

"No. No. It's just a little…" I paused to try to think of the right word. I didn't think there was one, but I would try. "Overwhelming."

And I've been having to put Todd and Henry off. They're getting impatient. It isn't as if I planned on dating only Mark. His showing up with the expectation that I would just go with him has been annoying. If he wasn't such a hunk, I might've turned him down just to prove a point.

I almost checked my cell phone to see if Todd had called again, but stopped myself just in time. Mark didn't like me checking my phone when he was with me.

"It's my charming good looks, isn't it?" His voice interrupted my thoughts.

I laughed and pushed back my chair. Mark handed me the huge vase of roses he'd been holding. I placed it on the desk then picked up the wilting arrangement. My heart gave a little twinge as I dumped the old bouquet in the trash so I'd have room for the new one. It had kept me company for the past week.

I leaned over the roses and took a deep breath. "Oooh. They smell amazing." I stepped up on tiptoe and kissed Mark's cheek. I didn't think a peck on the cheek counted as a real kiss. "Thanks for the roses." I enthused. I shut down my computer and headed out of my back office.

Leslie looked up as we walked by. Her light brown hair was pulled back in a tight bun. She glared at me through thick lenses, the solid black frame looking as rigid as her straight back. "Did you get that manuscript finished?"

"There's one more chapter. Do you want me to come in early tomorrow?"

"No. I can finish it first thing in the morning." Leslie turned back to her computer, her attention riveted to the screen.

As we stepped out into the hallway, Mark whispered, "She sure is surly."

"She's had a tough life."

"I can tell."

"How?"

"Every time I walk in, she looks like she wants to throw a book at me...or maybe her whole computer." Mark shuddered.

"You're just paranoid." I laughed.

"No. I'm serious. If looks could kill, I would have died right there in the front office the first time she met me."

"That's because before you came, I always stayed a few minutes after to finish up my projects," I admitted.

"You don't owe them any more time than your allotted four hours."

"I know, but I hate leaving loose ends."

"It isn't like you're going to make a career out of working in the Health Sciences Department."

My hackles rose at his unhappy tone. "Maybe not, but I like doing the very best I can at whatever I do."

Mark didn't reply. He was heading across the parking lot to his car. I never could get used to his breakneck pace.

Breathless, I asked, "Could you slow down a little?"

Mark looked down at me in surprise. "I don't want to be late for our reservation."

"You know what time I get out of work. Maybe you could make the reservation for five minutes later."

We'd reached his car by then, so he stopped while he opened his car. "I know your time is valuable. I'm trying to streamline our dates so you can get home and study."

His statement didn't quite ring true since he'd been just like this on our first date before he even knew I didn't like to go out on weekdays. *Whatever.* I thought. *It's not worth arguing about.*

As we drove the short distance to Los Hermanos, I mulled over what he'd been saying in my office. "What special activity did you have in mind?"

"I thought we'd stroll around the temple grounds."

Stroll? Did he say stroll? I didn't think he had that word in his vocabulary. Maybe he meant jog. "Sounds...fun." I glanced at Mark, a wrinkle forming between my brows in a question. "Why the temple?"

"I don't know." He shot a glance at me then turned to watch the road. "My roommate was telling me the fall

70

flowers look nice. It won't be long before it starts to snow and the flowers will be dug up for the winter."

"I haven't seen the fall gardens. Sounds nice." I stared out the window at the passing storefronts on University Avenue. *What does he really have in mind? I can't imagine Mark has any interest whatsoever in the fall gardens at the Provo Temple.*

After we were seated at the same table we'd sat at on our second date, I was relieved to see our server wasn't Dan. The new waiter's name was Brian. I wouldn't have blamed Dan if he spat in our food.

I had learned over the past few weeks that Mark didn't believe in tipping. He didn't seem to realize how little restaurant staff were paid. Most of their income came from tips, and I was tempted to start carrying extra cash around to leave tips of my own, but I didn't want to embarrass Mark, either. I stifled a sigh. *How long am I going to let him dictate my treatment of others?* I paused at the thought then answered myself. *Until I feel like he won't take my behavior as a slight against him. How long that will be, I have no idea.*

I glanced at Mark, then concentrated on the menu. After eating out with him every weekday for the past month, I'd discovered I didn't mind being adventurous. I had thought Mexican food meant tacos and burritos. After four weeks of eating out every day, I knew better. When Brian delivered our drinks, I ordered a chimichanga.

After Brian left, I reached out to touch Mark's hand. "I wanted to thank you for all the help you've been with my Spanish."

He smiled. "I've enjoyed our time together." He paused, a question forming in his eyes. "How did you do on your exam?"

I couldn't hide my delight. "I aced it, thanks to you."

"I wasn't the one taking the test."

71

"I'm serious. I couldn't have done it without you. You're a very good teacher." I meant it. He had been. Every time we met to study Spanish, he'd concentrated on the Spanish. After I'd made my position clear on how I felt about kissing, Mark hadn't even tried. I often wondered if he was getting his kisses somewhere else, but I didn't think he had too much time for anyone else. He was spending far too much of his spare time with me.

After we finished dinner, I hurried out of the restaurant after Mark. I didn't want to stick around and see the disappointed look on the waiter's face when he didn't get the tip he deserved.

The trip to the Provo Temple grounds was made with our usual lack of conversation. A few pairs of missionaries were playing catch in the field next to the Temple. I couldn't help the little thrill that went up my back seeing so many missionaries in one place. After growing up in Kansas, it seemed like a dream to be living within walking distance of not only a temple but also the Missionary Training Center.

Mark glanced over at me when I shivered. "What are you thinking about?"

"I was just excited to see the missionaries."

He chuckled. "If I hadn't grown up in California, I wouldn't know what you're talking about." He nodded at the group of missionaries playing in the field. "This never gets old."

I sighed happily. "I know. It's awesome."

Mark had put his car on autopilot as we left the restaurant. Since the temple was closed on Mondays, he knew he didn't have to worry about parking.

We stepped out of the car and walked—strolled, to my surprise—around the temple grounds.

Peace permeated the atmosphere. I noticed Mark was wearing his citrus and musk blend. He had four scents he wore. That one was my favorite.

As we walked through the grounds, I didn't feel like I should talk above a whisper. "You were right. The flower gardens are beautiful."

Mark led me to a secluded bench overlooking the temple grounds and the valley floor below. "Christina, I have something to ask you."

Suddenly, I felt like putting my hands over my ears and running like a five-year-old kid. *Why am I feeling this way?* I asked myself. *You know what he wants to ask. It's too soon. Too soon. We hardly know each other.* I controlled a desire to shudder and sat very still instead.

Mark paused, his gray eyes looking deep into mine.

I should be thrilled. He's everything I dreamed of. Why am I feeling like this? I asked myself again.

"Christina," he pulled out a ring box and opened it to reveal a full carat diamond ring, but it wasn't the diamond that made my eyes go big. It was the gold. There was enough gold in the ring to buy a car. No one bought gold rings these days, and knowing Mark, it wasn't fake. It would be real gold. "Will you marry me?"

"I...I don't know what to say." I stuttered.

"Surely you've seen this coming. We've spent every spare moment together."

"Yes, we have, but this is just our one month anniversary. We haven't known each other very long."

"I knew the moment we met you were the one for me."

How could he know that? I wondered. "I'm..." *what's the right word?* "touched." I could tell by his expression that I'd picked the wrong word, but I couldn't take it back. *What word would he want me to use?* "Honored." *There. He looks happier.* "I'm honored that you would choose me to be your wife. I…I was thinking I'd like to get married in the Manti Temple."

"Manti? Why Manti?"

"It was the assigned temple of the Salina Ward before the Temple in Winter Quarters was built. My grandparents were married in that temple."

"I believe it's closed for renovations until next year. I was hoping we could get married before then."

"When…when did you have in mind?" I hated stumbling over my words, but I was having a hard time wrapping my brain around his proposal. *Aren't people supposed to date a while before they get engaged?*

"I wanted to get married right after this semester. I always wanted a winter wedding."

My brain couldn't function. I couldn't do the math. "So how long would that give us to plan a wedding?"

"About two months?"

I wasn't sure Mark could see the look of horror on my face. "Two months to plan a wedding?"

Mark chuckled and touched my cheek. "It's been done before. Mormon weddings aren't hard to throw together. Three of my siblings have had quick weddings. It worked out just fine for Jeanette." He paused, a cunning gleam entering his eye. "Of course, it doesn't hurt that my dad bribes us with $25,000 if we keep the wedding preparations short and sweet."

"Oh." What was I supposed to say? $25,000 was an incentive to get married fast. It might even pay for the ring. But that meant my future father-in-law didn't mind throwing around money to get his way. It also meant I wouldn't get to plan the wedding of my dreams.

Was I willing to give all that up? Would my mother be willing to give it up? I didn't plan on ever marrying again. I wanted my one and only wedding to be spectacular, and I'd had plans in my head for years. I stifled a sigh. A Mormon wedding was, indeed, different. I'd been told the temple ceremony was short and simple. Maybe I didn't want my reception to outshine the wedding, after all.

I looked up at Mark. His beautiful gray eyes held a question. "Mark, this is a very important decision. I'd like to pray about it before I give you an answer."

He shut the ring box with an angry snap. "Take your time. Just remember, there are plenty of other women out there who would love to be in your shoes."

As if I need that reminder, I thought.

Chapter 7, Decision

The ride back to my dorm was quiet. Mark seethed.

Why is he so angry? Surely he wants me to know the Lord supports our union. I can't make a decision this big without consulting Him.

I snuck a peek at Mark's rigid profile and stifled a sigh. *Maybe he expected that I would have prayed about it already. He must think I'm desperate or something.* I felt indignant at that thought. *I know I haven't told him about my other dates, but he must not think much of me if he thinks I don't have any other prospects.*

I tried to stay angry with Mark, but even his fuming profile was handsome. I was infatuated. I knew it. Nan knew it. My parents knew it. I stifled another sigh. *How am I going to know if my answer is my own or the Lord's? How will I know?*

When the car stopped in front of the dorm, I was startled. I hadn't been paying any attention to where we were.

Mark didn't bother to follow me to the dorm. I wasn't surprised.

Nan hadn't returned from her study session when I arrived in my room. I was relieved. I needed some time alone. And some time on the phone.

Mom picked up the phone on the second ring. "Hi, Sweetie, what's up?"

"Mark proposed."

"He what?"

"He proposed."

"But you've only known each other a month." Her stress was audible. I held the phone from my ear.

"I know, Mom." I sat on the bed and traced the bold pattern. "I'm trying to decide what my answer will be."

We were both quiet for a moment and I continued to trace the pattern with an idle finger.

Mom broke the silence. "I...I don't know what to say. How are you feeling about

about all this?"

"I want to say yes, Mom. You know how much I like Mark."

Even though we were separated by more than a thousand miles, I could picture my mom nodding her head. I'd spent enough time extolling Mark's virtues over the past month that Mom knew my feelings on the matter. "Yes. I know you're infatuated. But..."

"Infatuation doesn't last. I know. You've told me that before. So, Mom, how did you know Dad was *the* one for you? I mean, what kinds of feelings did you have?"

She paused a moment, then continued softly, "Well, I saw how Dad treated you. I liked how respectful he was with me. Mostly, though, it was how peaceful I felt when we were together."

I drew my brows together in a puzzled frown. "So, when you're with the one you're supposed to be with, you feel peace?"

"Yes, you do." Mom's voice was firm.

"Don't you feel anything else? Like your heart thumping wildly or something?"

Mom's voice changed. I could hear her smile. "Well, there is some of that, yes." Then her voice grew serious again. "It's important to feel some kind of...I don't know...physical attraction...for the person you want to spend eternity with, but you can have that kind of feeling for anyone. If he's not a worthy priesthood holder, those kinds of feelings don't matter. He won't be a good husband and father. That's why Dad and I wouldn't let you date non-members. Being married in the temple is too important to risk your falling in love with someone who can't take you there."

"Mark can take me to the temple, but I just want to be sure I'm making the right decision. Forever is a long time."

Mom's voice took on a cautious tone. "Sweetie, only you can make that kind of decision. We aren't the ones who will be living with it. Whatever you decide, Dad and I will support you. If you're feeling confused, you can make a list of his strengths and weaknesses. Pay attention to your feelings. They matter."

I bit my lip. I wanted Mom to help me out, and she was throwing it all "plop" right back into my own lap. I swallowed a lump, but I couldn't hide the sound of unshed tears. "Thanks, Mom. I'll do that."

"I'm sorry, Sweetie, I know you wanted something more…"

"No. It's okay. You're right. I'll puzzle it out somehow."

"Call me back when you've made your decision."

"I will. Love you, Mom."

"Love you more."

A smile emerged as I shut the phone. Talking to Mom hadn't fixed my problem, but it reminded me she would always be there.

I knelt beside my bed and begged for an answer. The only thought that entered was *"this kind goeth not out but by prayer and fasting."* I knew the scripture reference. It came from Matthew 17:21. *What kind of thought is that?*

I pondered a moment. *Maybe it means I need to fast about my decision.* I prayed a second time. This time, it was to start a fast. I would ask the Lord again after I'd been fasting a day. Maybe I'd get a clearer answer then.

After spending some time studying for the music exam the following morning, I looked up from my desk as Nan arrived. She quickly changed into her pajamas. We shared a brief prayer then she dropped into bed, exhausted. Her schedule was even more grueling than mine. As usual, we didn't spend much time chatting. I was grateful for it that night. My mind was so full, I didn't think I could form a coherent sentence.

When Nan dropped into her bed, I took my turn in the bathroom. Hot steam from the shower billowed around the room, but it didn't calm my troubled heart. I wanted an answer, and it wasn't coming like I wanted. I stepped out of the shower. If the mirror hadn't been fogged with steam, I was sure I would've seen a lobster-red reflection. I worked through the knots in my curls and tried to think. Whenever I tried to create a mental list of Mark's good traits and bad traits, his beautiful gray eyes filled my mind. Frustrated, I dropped the brush on the counter with a clatter and headed back into my room.

I settled into bed with a sigh. Beams of light from passing cars chased themselves across the ceiling. After tossing and turning for endless hours, I drifted into a troubled sleep.

I groaned as I reached for the alarm the following morning. My exhausted body didn't want to move. Then I remembered it was my music exam day. I groaned again and rolled out of bed, my bare feet slapping against the cold linoleum.

Nan was rolled up in her own covers. She was still there, wrapped up like a cocoon, when I emerged from the bathroom a few minutes later. I didn't bother putting much makeup on. It wouldn't have hidden the circles under my eyes, anyway.

Mark won't call today. I surprised myself with the thought. *He wants me to come crawling back.* I paused a moment, pondering what those thoughts meant, then finished dressing. It bothered me that I thought Mark wanted me to crawl. That meant he expected a subservient attitude, and I'd never been one to accept that role.

I managed to get through the quiz in my music class without much trouble. Remembering different tempos and types of music was getting easier as the class progressed.

Every time my stomach growled or my mouth felt parched, I prayed about my decision. By the time I was walking out the door of my office, I was no nearer an answer. The fragrance of the flowers Mark had dropped off the evening before hadn't helped my concentration. How could I think with the scent of his gift perfuming the air? The roses reminded me of his virile presence and his glorious gray eyes. I was no nearer thinking up a list of pros and cons than I had been the night before. I sighed as I shut and locked the door.

The dorm room was empty when I arrived. I sat at my desk and filled out a two-column table. "Good Traits" and "Bad Traits" topped the columns.

The first thing I wrote under "Good Traits" was "Loves the Lord." Surely anyone who served a two-year mission had that trait. I continued down the list. "Honors Priesthood." "Active in the Church." I assumed he was active since he was attending BYU, although I'd never visited his ward. "Loves Family." I saw that from how he treated his sister and her family. Since this was my own list and no one else would see it, I decided to include traits that didn't have eternal significance. "Gorgeous Eyes." "Thick, curly hair." "Always smells nice." The thought of his four

81

different colognes had my lips twitching. "Sexy." I blushed when I remembered all the times he'd tried to touch me.

I sat back and chewed on my pencil. Those were the only traits I could think of. I bent over the paper to write down his "Bad Traits." "Walks too fast." His habit of practically running everywhere he went had annoyed me on our first date. It still annoyed me. "Won't tip." I bit my lip. That was one I almost couldn't live with. "Paranoid." The way he thought my boss was always after him was almost funny. I tapped the eraser of my pencil on the page and tried to add something more to the list. As I stared at it a moment, I realized all three traits could be summarized in a single sentence: "Doesn't love his neighbor as himself." *What a horrible thought.* I ripped the paper out of the notebook, wadded it into a ball, and tossed it angrily into the wastebasket.

I stared unseeingly at the small bulletin board. Even the smiling face of my family staring from the familiar photograph didn't help me focus. *I'm broken. I can't feel things right. My...* I couldn't help a shudder...*creation won't let me be normal. How can I hear the Lord if I'm not even supposed to be here?* I stopped myself and remembered all the wonderful things Garrett—my real dad—had done for me and my mom. I never once felt like I didn't belong, so why was I having these feelings?

I knelt to pray about my decision with Mark and to break my fast. When silence was my answer, I rose to my feet. *God isn't listening. I should've never been born. Why should he listen? My father was a beast. I was created by a monster. Why would God listen to me?*

The second Article of Faith flashed through my mind. "We believe that men will be punished for their own sins, and not for Adam's transgression." I rolled my eyes. Why would an article I learned in Primary suddenly pop into my head? It had nothing to do with marrying Mark.

I stomped out of the room, shutting the door with enough force to make the hinges shake.

When I entered the cafeteria for dinner, I was astonished to see Nan sitting by herself at a corner table. After I filled my tray, I moved to join her.

She looked up in surprise. "No Mark?"

I shook my head. "He's busy tonight. I thought you'd be eating with Todd."

"He went to dinner with someone he met in his religion class."

My heart felt like it was being rung out like a wet washrag. The intensity of my feelings stunned me. *Why should I even care? Mark should be the one on my mind, not Todd. We've never even held hands. He treats me like a sister. Why shouldn't Todd date?*

Nan was watching my expression intently, like she was trying to see what this announcement meant to me. I kept my expression carefully neutral. How and when Todd dated shouldn't even matter.

"I already blessed the food." Nan offered.

I nodded. I figured she had. Nan was careful about her religious observations. I tended to get lax about prayer when it was in public. Nan never let her location affect how she treated God. I wished I could be more like her.

I shook out my napkin and placed it on my lap. The smell rising from my plate made my mouth water, but the first bite was like sawdust. My emotions were in too much turmoil for me to distinguish flavors. Suddenly, I wished for a bite of the jalapeño salsa from Los Hermanos. It would have sliced through my haze. Maybe that's why Mark liked it so much. Intense flavor held you in the moment.

Even though I'd been fasting for 24 hours, I pushed away from the table after a few bites. Food had no meaning when I wanted an answer. "I'm heading to bed."

Nan looked up from her own meal. "Are you feeling well?"

I shook my head. "I think I'm coming down with something." *A case of the Mark Sandstrom blues.*

"I'm so sorry. Would you like me to ask Todd to come and give you a blessing?"

I opened my eyes wide in horror. I couldn't imagine Todd coming over and giving me a blessing for the kind of illness I was experiencing. "No. It's okay. I'm sure I'll be fine in the morning."

Nan looked doubtful. "Alright, if you say so."

I walked back to my room and knelt again to pray.

My mind filled with images of Mark. From our first rushed date where I met Jeanette, who I had come to love dearly, to the next day when Mark's breath had tickled my neck when he asked for another date, to all the times we'd laughed through meals. I thought about the lovely flowers he'd left in my office. His delicious variety of scents. Why shouldn't I be his wife? If he was proud to have me at his side, why shouldn't I be the one standing there?

"Thou shalt love thy neighbor as thyself," whispered in my mind. Angrily, I pushed the message out of my head. *I am the daughter of a rapist. God doesn't speak to me. I will make this decision myself.*

Before I could talk myself out of the choice I had made, I dialed Mark's number. To my surprise, he didn't pick up the phone. For a split second, an image of Mark making out with the gorgeous redhead sitting two chairs away from us in Physics entered my head. I shoved that image away and spoke into his voicemail box. "Mark, I've taken some time to fast and pray about this decision. I'd be delighted to be your wife. When did you want to get married?" I shut the phone and stared at it a moment. *Mom wants to know what I've decided. I...I just can't call her tonight.* I couldn't explain my mixed feelings. *This doesn't feel like the peace Mom talked about. I don't know if I can feel peace. What does it feel like, anyway? How will I know when I get my answer? Maybe something is wrong with me.* A hot shower did little to dissipate the troubling thoughts tumbling through my head.

I was wrapped up in my bedding an hour later when Nan quietly entered the room. She must've believed my story about feeling ill because she felt her way to the bathroom before turning on the light then walked back to shut the door. She was trying hard to let me sleep. I could feel the flush of guilt warm my face and was glad she hadn't turned on the light in the main room. My red cheeks would've given away my sleepless state. I stifled a sigh.

Several minutes later, Nan settled into her own bed. Her steady breathing soon told me she was sleeping. I hadn't yet heard her struggle to get to sleep. I wondered what her secret was. Maybe it had something to do with treating her God the same no matter where she was. I stifled another sigh. *I need to be more like her.*

I rolled to my side and stared at the blinds. Light flashed through the slats as cars moved up and down the street. A blue light flashed across the blind. It came from LED headlights. I had the distinct impression the headlights belonged to Mark's car. *What a stupid idea.* I rolled away from the blinds and forced my eyes shut. The hours of struggling to seek an answer had worn me out. I fell into a dreamless sleep.

I straightened my shoulders before opening the door to the physics class. I wasn't sure how stepping through that door would impact the rest of my life, but I was sure it would have some kind of significance.

Mark was staring at the professor, who was shuffling through papers at the podium. The class didn't start for another five minutes.

He's ignoring me. I gritted my teeth. *He's getting on my last nerve. If this is some kind of game, I don't like how he plays it.*

Mark looked up when I sat down next to him. I couldn't read his expression. His eyes were shuttered.

"Did you get my message?" I asked.

He nodded.

"Well...did you decide on a date?"

He nodded again. I fought a desire to roll my eyes. He wasn't acting like a thrilled suitor.

Finally, he leaned over and moved my hair away from my ear. Despite my annoyance, a thrill shot through me as his breath warmed my neck. "December 21. It's the week after finals. Does that sound okay?"

I tried to remember what my plans were for December, but I drew a blank. His touch wiped out coherent thought. I watched the professor, who looked like she was about to speak. I whispered. "That sounds great." I turned to Mark, a furrow between my brows. "When were you planning to meet my parents?"

"Your parents?" His shocked look was a surprise. *Surely he wasn't planning a wedding without first having met my parents?*

I nodded. "I've been talking about you so much, I'm sure they feel they know you already, but I'd like you to meet my family before the wedding."

The professor started into her lecture, and Mark faced the front. He folded his arms across his chest and pointed his long legs away from me.

I bit my lip. I couldn't imagine that my needing to pray about the decision should be something he would feel angry about. And his shock at my wanting him to meet my

86

family was a complete surprise. I'd already met his sister. We spent every Sunday with her and her family. Why wouldn't he want to meet my family? And shouldn't I meet his parents as well? A short engagement was one thing. A complete disregard for the blending of two families was something else.

I tried to ignore Mark's stony face as the professor's lecture continued. It was a long hour, and I wasn't sure I absorbed anything from the droning voice at the front of the class. As the other students started to gather their backpacks for the trek across campus, I was surprised to see that I had scribbled a few notes across my paper. *I hope they'll help me pass the exam.*

The redhead I'd envisioned with Mark the night before paused to smile coyly at Mark. *What does that mean?* flashed across my mind, but I was too wrapped up in his behavior to pay much attention to her.

"So…have you decided when you can meet my folks?" I asked.

"I was thinking we could go over Halloween weekend." He replied.

I opened my eyes wide in surprise. "That's only a couple of weeks away."

"It shouldn't be a problem. We can fly."

"Isn't that expensive?" My brows furrowed with concern.

He chuckled. "I think my bank account can handle it."

I wondered *If flying out to Kansas isn't a problem, why can't he pay a decent tip?* Hiding my thoughts, I asked, "Which airport were you planning to land at?"

"Which one is closer to Salina?"

The Salina airport is too small to host a flight from Salt Lake. "Probably the Wichita airport. Kansas City is four hours away. Wichita is only two."

"Wichita it is, then."

"Did you want me to make the flight arrangements?" I asked.

"No." Mark shook his head. "I'll be paying for the tickets, so I'll handle it."

I breathed a sigh of relief. I'd never purchased airline tickets. I wasn't sure what the procedure was—especially since I wasn't the one paying.

Mark's smile lit up his face. "I'll meet you after Spanish class for our usual tutoring session."

"I'm looking forward to it." *How am I supposed to act? Are we really engaged? How am I supposed to treat him?*

Mark treated me the same way he'd been treating me for weeks. We held hands on the walk to Spanish class and Mark handed over my backpack. He reached out to stop me when I started to head into class. "I forgot to give you this." He pulled out the small velvet box that contained the engagement ring. With a twinge of disappointment, I realized he wasn't going to get on his knee and beg me to be his wife. He simply opened the box. "Here. Let's see if this fits."

I held out my left hand. The ring slid on as if it was made for me. The gold was heavier than I anticipated. I held out the ring to admire the flashing diamond. The gold band was solid and wide. For a fleeting moment, it felt like a fettering band, but I pushed that feeling aside as I stepped on tiptoe to administer a quick peck on his cheek. Mark didn't protest. I'd already made my position clear. "Thanks. I love you."

"You're welcome." He smiled down at me then walked away. I stared at his disappearing back, astonished that he hadn't once said "I love you."

The Spanish class was a blur. My mind was full of Mark. I couldn't help but wonder what kind of husband he would make if he couldn't even blurt out "I love you" when he'd made a proposal of marriage. *He must be as nervous as I am. It's new for both of us. That's all. I'm sure he loves me. He wouldn't have proposed unless he did.*

After Spanish class, Mark met me at the door. He led me at his usual breakneck pace to the library where we had a room set aside for tutoring. I suspected he had it scheduled through the rest of the semester, but I hadn't asked. To my surprise, our study session ran the same way it always did as if our situation hadn't changed at all. As we wrapped up our time together, I touched Mark's arm and looked up into his eyes. "Mark, you seem...I don't know...distracted. Are you sure you want to go through with this?"

His eyes warmed as he looked into mine. "Of course I do. Jeanette told me the first day she met you that she thought you'd make a great wife. You're beautiful, you're intelligent, and we get along well."

I controlled a desire to roll my eyes. He sounded like he was checking off items on a list. I wanted to know if he loved me. I stifled a sigh. Maybe I had been a little hasty in having a goal of no kissing until over the altar. *Maybe a kiss will make a difference.*

I was no expert, but I'd watched enough movies to figure out how things went. We were all alone in a small room with just one window. I stepped over to Mark while he was ticking off his list and pulled his head down to mine. "I love you, Mark," I whispered then met his warm lips with mine. He didn't argue. It would have been useless, anyway. I wasn't taking "no" for an answer. His lips gently caressed mine and then grew more urgent. Finally, I pulled away gasping, my eyes wide. I'd never been kissed, and I hadn't known what to expect. Having my whole body light up in response to his moving lips wasn't something I'd expected. *Wow.*

Mark smiled down at me, a fire I didn't understand smoldering in their depths. "What was that for? I thought you wanted to wait until over the altar."

"I…I don't know what came over me. I guess…" and I traced his jaw tenderly, "I just wanted to be sure you love me."

Roughly, he caught me in another embrace and traced my cheek and down my throat with fiery kisses. When he reached the hollow of my throat, someone came bursting in through the door.

"Christina, Nan said you'd be here. You haven't been answering my calls…" Todd's voice trailed off as I stepped back from Mark. Todd quickly switched gears. "I'm sorry, I didn't know you were with someone." Todd glared at Mark, as if he had some claim on me.

"I'm s-sorry." I stammered. "Todd is my roommate's brother." I made introductions. "Todd…this is my fiancé, Mark."

"How long have you known this…this…this…" My eyes grew wide. Todd's stuttering rage was a shock.

"I met him about three weeks after school started. Hasn't Nan told you we've been dating?" I answered.

"Yes, but you've only been dating a month. We went out before you ever met Mark."

"You're Nan's brother, Todd. I didn't think that counted as a date." I protested.

Todd's eyes were narrow slits. "I'm sorry you feel that way, Christina. I don't share the same opinion." With that cryptic comment, he turned on his heel and shut the door behind him. The door shook with the force of his anger.

Mark cocked his head and furrowed his brow. "Who did you say that was?"

I sighed. "Todd Cohen, Nan's brother."

He raised his brows. "Did you know he had a thing for you?"

I shook my head, my long curls swinging in unison. "I had no idea. I thought he just considered me one of Nan's friends—like a sister. I had no idea he had any interest at all."

Todd's revelation was a shock. I couldn't imagine it would change how I felt. Mark held every waking thought. I didn't have room for anyone else.

"Where to tonight?" Mark asked.

I glanced up from my computer, surprised at his request. That was a first. "Umm..." I tried to think of some place we hadn't been for a while. "I feel like something light. I'd just like a salad at the CougarEat, if you don't mind." An image of my first meal there flashed in my mind. Todd's twinkling eyes tore at my heart when I remembered they'd been replaced by eyes full of hurt and anger when he'd burst in on us earlier.

"Whatever you want. It's an easy walk from here." Mark's voice brought me back to the moment.

He pulled me into his arms and bent his head for what began as a passionate kiss. I pulled away quickly. Mark's brows furrowed. "What's wrong?"

"I...I'd rather keep our kisses short and sweet. I'd like to make it to the temple in December."

Mark smirked. "That won't be a problem with your attitude."

I closed my eyes and sighed, then looked up at him. "You're positively dangerous. I need to keep my distance."

Without arguing, Mark waited for me to shut down the computer then reached for my hand. His hand always felt comfortable, like my hand was meant to fit into his. For one moment, I wondered what it would be like to hold

Todd's hand. I suppressed the thought as I followed Mark out the door.

After dinner, Mark dropped me off at the dorm. Nan was writing, as she usually did when she was in her room by herself.

"What are you writing?" I asked. I hadn't voiced my curiosity before.

"My journal."

"You seem pretty intense about it."

She looked up at me. "I'm only going to be mortal once. I want to be able to keep a record so I can refer to it throughout the eternities."

I stared at her a moment, then blurted out. "I never thought of it that way. I guess I should be writing in mine, too."

"The prophets have made it clear. It's a mandate."

That, of course, was the end of the discussion for her. I'd never met someone who was so careful to follow every commandment.

I kicked off my shoes and sat cross legged in the middle of my bed. After watching Nan write for a couple of minutes, I blurted out, "I'm getting married."

The lead on Nan's pencil broke. A deep furrow formed between her brows. "Wh-what did you say?"

"I said. . . I'm getting married."

"Does Todd know?"

What an odd question. "Yes. I told him today."

"How did he take it?"

I shrugged. "I don't know…he seemed upset."

Nan stared at me a moment, bit her lip, then pulled out another pencil and continued her writing. She didn't look up. I sighed. She wasn't going to spend any more time discussing the matter.

A couple of days later, I picked up a call from Henry.

"Hi, Christina? I haven't had any time with all the tests I've been taking. Sorry I've been neglecting you."

I bit my lip. I wasn't sure how I was going to break the news. *Here goes nothing.* "No problem, Henry. I've been busy myself. In fact, I'm getting married on December 21."

"You're what?" Henry's voice held all the disbelief of Nan's reaction.

"I'm engaged. I'm getting married on December 21."

"How long have you known this guy?"

I swallowed a chuckle. "I met him after we went to that movie together."

"That's only been like… a month?"

"He swept me off my feet. What can I say?"

"Wow. I guess he did. Lucky guy." He paused, as if trying to figure out a safe way to get out of our conversation. "My roommate's dad owns a jewelry store. He can get you a good deal on a ring."

"That's awesome. I wish I would've known. Mark already got me one, but thanks for the heads up."

"Yeah. Well. Good luck. I wish you the best." I could hear he meant it. *Poor Henry.*

"Thanks. I appreciate it." I almost said *keep in touch.* "I enjoyed our time together, Henry. Thanks for the fun times." *Two dates. Fun times. How long will it be before I forget all about him?* I surprised myself with another thought. *Never. I'll always remember him.* And I knew it was true. His cheery dimple had touched my soul.

Chapter 8, Peppy

N ervous?" Mark asked.

I nodded. "I haven't ever been in a plane."

"It's safer than highway travel—even with so many cars having autopilot, there are still enough idiots on the road that it's a slaughterhouse out there."

I shuddered. I didn't like thinking about people dying anywhere, and car accidents were particularly ugly.

My knuckles were white as I gripped the armrests. I was grateful for the room in first class. The seats in the back part of the plane didn't have individual armrests. I would've been sharing the armrest with my neighbor. I glanced at Mark, who sat relaxed in his seat. Of course, my neighbor would've been Mark, so it wouldn't have been that bad. He didn't seem to need to grip the seat like I did.

Non-stop prayer filled my mind as the plane lifted up in the air. I'd heard the most dangerous part of flying was taking off and landing. The ground shrank beneath the wings. I stared out the window as the plane banked and headed east. After we leveled out, I relaxed my grip on the seat and flexed my frozen fingers.

Mark chuckled. "I thought you were going to rip the armrests right off the seat."

"Was it that bad?"

He nodded at my flexing fingers. "Yeah. It was pretty obvious."

I sighed. "Sorry. This is all new to me." I stared out the window. "I've never seen Utah from this perspective. It looks almost empty."

"It's not a very populated state, but even California looks empty when you're flying over the Central Valley."

I couldn't imagine California with its swarms of people looking empty, but I'd never flown over it, either.

About half an hour into the flight, my head found a comfortable spot on Mark's shoulder. I slept through most of it.

Mark's gentle shaking and "Wake up, Sleepy Head. We're getting ready to land," combined to rouse me from a dreaming state.

I sat up and yawned. "I'm so sorry. I didn't mean to fall asleep."

"That's all right. I know you've been working hard on your studies."

I stretched and yawned again, then made sure my seat was upright for landing. I stared out the window as the plane circled over Wichita to head into the runway. Miles of farm fields stretched out beyond the city limits. "Have you ever seen so many farms?"

Mark looked over my shoulder. "The Central Valley in California looks a lot like this—acres of farmland stretching out to the horizon."

I stared out the window a few more minutes until the tilt of the plane told me the plane was heading for the runway. I stared ahead and reached for the armrests. I couldn't control the fear that gripped me.

Mark patted my hand, as if trying to comfort me then stared out the window to watch the approaching tarmac. He obviously didn't share my fear of flying. *At least he's not laughing at me*, I thought.

"Thank you for flying United Air. I hope you enjoyed the flight." The pilot announced from the cockpit. "Wichita

weather is sunny and 73°. Enjoy your stay and please fly
United next time you choose to fly."

I suppressed a shudder. I knew I'd be flying again in a
couple of days. I wasn't looking forward to it.

As we stepped into the terminal, I pulled my cell phone
out of my purse and dialed Mom. She picked up on the
second ring. "Hi, Mom."

"Hi, Sweetie. How was the flight?"

"Uneventful, thank goodness. We've landed. We
should be at the curb in ten minutes."

"I'll be there."

"Okay, Mom. Thanks for coming to pick us up."

"No problem. I love you."

Ever since his proposal, Mark had tried to make an
effort to walk slower. I was grateful he'd finally heard me.
Mark reached for my hand and led me over to the luggage
carousel, where our bags were already being dumped from
the conveyor belt onto the metal turntable. A large black
bag with its handle wrapped in pink duct tape headed our
way. "That's mine."

Mark reached out to grab it then found his black bag.
The rich black leather was a stark contrast to the polyester
cover of my own bag. As they sat next to each other, I
wondered if people could see the difference between Mark
and I just as clearly. I wasn't raised in the opulent
surroundings Mark had apparently been raised in. *Am I
really Mark's equal?* The thought burned in my mind.

"Where to?" Mark's voice broke into my thoughts.

"Mom is meeting us at the curb."

When Mom drove up in the Suburban, I could see the
faces of my brothers and sisters pressed against the
windows. They'd wriggled out of their seatbelts in their
eagerness to see Mark.

I smiled and waved.

"Wow. Your mom brought the whole crew." Mark sounded surprised.

"Everyone but Dad. It's hard for him to get away if there's a client needing help."

A babble of voices met us as the door opened. I couldn't understand any of it, but I felt like a wave of love had enveloped me. This was home. It didn't matter that we weren't in Salina yet.

Mom's voice rose over the others. "Sit down and buckle up. We can visit with Mark and Christina one at a time. You're giving me a headache." The noise quieted to the sound of clicking seat belts.

"Thanks, Mom," I breathed then reached over for a hug.

The back of the SUV opened so Mark could stow the luggage. He climbed in next to Tobias, who was waving at him with a sticky sucker.

The doors shut with a click. Mom pulled into traffic. Salina was a little under two hours away.

The conversation quickly turned to wedding plans. Mom and I talked non-stop the entire trip.

My siblings were entranced with Mark. He answered their questions and turned to look at whatever passing item of interest was pointed out. *Jeanette's kids have taught him well.* I thought. My heart soared with happiness. Mark was fitting in.

When we pulled up to the house, the familiar shape of our three-story house tugged at my heart. I'd missed the old place.

Bounding up to meet us was Peppy, his black pirate eye patch and floppy ear looking as comical as ever. We all piled out and headed to the house.

As Mark followed me, Peppy knocked him flat. Peppy's bared teeth were mere centimeters from Mark's face. His ferocious snarl was a shock.

"Peppy!" Mom's look of angry surprise was joined with my own. I'd never seen Peppy growl at anyone, much less knock them flat and look like he wanted to eat them for lunch.

Mark's eyes were narrow slits of rage. He growled through clenched teeth. "Get this *mongrel* off of me."

I joined my strength with Mom's as we strained on Peppy's collar. "Peppy, come on." I begged. With both of us pulling, we managed to get Peppy off Mark.

Mark stomped toward the house. Peppy took advantage of our momentary distraction and ripped out of our grasp. He charged after Mark, who decided it best to sprint. He yelped in pain as Peppy ripped into the seat of his pants. I bit my lip to keep the laughter from bubbling out. I couldn't speak while biting my lip, but I did race after the two of them.

I was afraid to look Mom in the eye. I knew if I did, we'd both be rolling on the lawn in helpless laughter. *Peppy snarling? Since when?*

We reached Peppy at the same time and held tight while Mark managed to make his escape into the house.

We walked Peppy around to the garage. When we managed to get him shut in, we caught each other's eyes. That did it. We burst out laughing and were soon doubled over. After a few minutes, I realized Mark would wonder where his fiancé had sequestered herself. "Mom," I whispered around tears of laughter, "please don't mention this to Mark." I giggled again. "I don't think he would be amused."

Mom wiped a tear of laughter out of her own eye then giggled with me. "Mum's the word." We both turned to stare at Peppy, who was standing on his hind legs and staring out the window of the garage door. His furious barking was muffled by the double-paned windows.

"Well, we know what he thinks about Mark." Mom turned and put her arm around me as we headed into the house. "Let's hope Dad has a better opinion."

Chapter 9, Salt Lake Temple

The remaining few weeks before the wedding were hectic.

Mark's parents had flown out the week after our visit with my family. I felt intimidated by them, but my attachment to Jeanette gave me hope that I would fit into his family.

I had to plan the wedding around study time, and that wasn't easy.

Mark continued to tutor me in Spanish. Without his help, I doubt I would've passed the Spanish class. Since we had already established a dating routine that included study time, we were able to maintain some order to our time together.

With the strict policy in place at the dorm, Mark never did come to my room, and I never entered his. It wasn't something I was interested in, and I'm not sure why. Maybe somewhere inside, I was scared of what I would see.

Dress shopping was problematic. Finally getting desperate, I entered a shop other classmates had told me was abominably expensive.

As I stepped into the shop, the fragrance of fresh flowers and the sharp scent of eucalyptus leaves filled the air. Mannequins were dressed in elaborate Cinderella dresses. Yards of fabric must've gone into the creation of each one. Lace and silks vied for attention. Veils, elbow length gloves, and a rainbow assortment of bridesmaids' gowns shared the sales floor with the wedding gowns.

What caught my attention were the gowns' designs. They were created with temple weddings in mind. All of them were temple ready. What a relief.

A sales associate approached me as I scanned the merchandise. "Hi. My name is Ellie. What can I help you with today?"

"Hello." I reached out to shake her hand. "I'm Christina. I'm getting married in the Salt Lake Temple on December 21, and I don't have a gown yet."

Her eyes widened as she released her firm clasp. "That's not much time."

"I know. Do you have anything that might fit me?"

She stepped back and looked me up and down. "I think we might have a few gowns. I'll go check for you."

As she walked to the back room to sift through her gowns, I worked my way around the sales floor and tried to look at the price tags without being too obvious about it.

I almost gasped aloud when I caught sight of a price tag. *Turn around and walk out,* was the thought that came to mind, but then I protested. *I don't have time to shop anywhere else.*

I walked over and picked up another tag. My heart sank. *How can Mom and Dad afford to pay this much for a gown? This would pay for an entire semester at BYU. What a waste of money.* I continued to argue with myself. *The wedding is only two weeks away. Mark will expect me to look like a successful lawyer's wife. I've already looked everywhere else. There isn't anything available.* I took a deep breath to calm myself then the thought came. *There's always Deseret Industries. I haven't checked there.* I ground my teeth together. *What a stupid idea. Mark would never be happy knowing we got married with me in a used gown.*

102

I looked up as Ellie approached with a tall stack of gowns cuddled in her arms. My eyes widened. *It looks like I'll be trying on gowns for a while.*

We walked into a changing room. Ellie followed me in and shut the door. My brows furrowed in a question.

"I thought you could use some help with the gowns." Ellie answered my unasked question.

"Thanks." I mumbled. *I really don't want a stranger watching me change, but she probably does this every day.*

Then I remembered Mom wasn't with me. *Most girls aren't all alone picking out a wedding gown.* My heart constricted, and I swallowed my tears. Doing all this in such a hurry was depriving me of the joy of sharing the moment with Mom.

Ellie helped me change into several gowns. To my surprise, she had chosen a perfect size for me. All the gowns fit.

After staring at my reflection through several changes of clothes, I decided on a simple gown that showed off my slim figure. "I like this one."

"Good choice," Ellie approved.

I'll bet she'd say that no matter what I picked. I bit my lip to hide a wry smile.

The blood drained from my face when I saw the price tag. It was almost double the price of the one I'd seen out on the sales floor. I couldn't imagine why the gown I picked was so much pricier than the other one. It didn't have nearly as much material. Then I remembered the name associated with the dress. In my desire to find something that didn't need altering, I'd picked a dress from a well-known designer. My heart sank.

No wonder Ellie liked my choice. Her commission will feed her for a month. Ugh. Maybe I should pick one of the other gowns. Before I could say anything, Ellie had already left the room with the other gowns draped over her arms.

Too embarrassed to make a switch, I picked up my cell phone and dialed a familiar number.

"Mom, I found the perfect dress today, but it costs a lot more than I planned to spend."

"Where at?"

"A bridal shop in Provo."

"Does it need altering?"

"I hunted for one that wouldn't need anything." I paused a moment, mentally counting down the days to the wedding. "We don't have any time for alterations."

Mom sighed. "That's true. How much is it?"

To my surprise, when I told her the price, she didn't protest. Instead, she said, "If you love it, you'd better buy it before someone else snatches it up." She paused a moment, then continued. "Are you sure Mark won't let us put off the wedding? I feel like there just isn't any time, and having an anniversary so close to Christmas will always be a problem."

I echoed Mom's sigh. "No. I'm sorry, Mom. Mark is dead set on that December 21st date."

"Did he ever give you a reason?"

I shook my head before remembering Mom couldn't see me. "No. He just said he always wanted a winter wedding."

"Did he even ask what kind of wedding you wanted?"

My voice took on a wry tone. "Somehow, that never entered the picture. I guess I didn't really care, as long as I got married in the temple."

I could hear the smile in Mom's voice. "I guess we did emphasize that point, didn't we?"

"Frequently." I laughed. "Well, we'll both be getting my temple wedding. I guess the rest doesn't matter so much."

"It doesn't, but I wanted you to know we got The Chapel reserved."

"You mean the reception building that used to be a stake center?"

"That's the one."

"Sweet. I didn't think it would be available on such short notice."

"We had to put down a sizeable chunk on deposit."

"Oh, Mom." I protested, "You and Dad shouldn't be spending so much."

"It's your only wedding, Christina. It's not like we can't afford it."

"It's not like you have tons of money to throw around, either." I protested again.

"We wanted to teach you kids restraint." I could hear Mom's smile again. "We have plenty set aside for weddings and missions. You don't need to worry that we'll be in the poor house any time soon."

I thought back to all the times Mom and Dad had refused to eat out or buy anything on the spur of the moment because we didn't have enough money. *They did that for us?* I suddenly realized Mom and Dad had sacrificed a great deal over the years to teach us valuable lessons. It was a revelation.

"I love you, Mom. Thanks for everything. Are you sure you want me to get this dress? Maybe I can find something at DI."

Mom laughed outright. "No, Christina. The money was set aside years ago. It's not going to hurt our budget. Your wedding is covered. You don't need to get a used dress for your wedding."

The weight off my shoulders was a tangible thing. I'd been more worried about the wedding expenses than I realized. "Thanks, Mom. Please tell Dad how much I appreciate this."

"We both want you to be happy, Christina. Despite Peppy's opinion," she paused while I snickered, "we think Mark is a fine young man, and we wish you all happiness."

"I guess I'll be seeing you in a couple of weeks. Are the kids coming?"

"Yes. We decided this event was too important not to fly everyone. We didn't want to chance driving with the weather being so uncertain this time of year. The kids are looking forward to their first flight."

I smiled at the thought. I could imagine how thrilled they would be to get to ride in an airplane. They'd probably feed off the novelty for months afterward. There weren't too many kids in Salina who had the opportunity to fly.

I had always wanted pictures with my siblings on the steps in front of the temple doors. *At least two of my dreams are coming true. Having my wedding in the temple is the most important one. Everything else is fluff.*

"Christina? Are you there?"

Mom's voice brought me out of my reverie. "Yes. I'm sorry, Mom. I was just thinking about all the money you're spending."

"Christina, don't worry about it. As I mentioned before, the money was set aside years ago. It's not impacting our budget. In fact, there will be some funds left over so you can continue your education, if you want."

"Wow. I had no idea. I really appreciate this, Mom."

"It's our pleasure. Really. We're so proud of you, Christina. We're all looking forward to sharing your special day."

Ellie walked into the room with an expectant expression. *She probably wants me to pay.*

"I'm going to buy the dress now, Mom. I'll call you back later."

"No problem. I love you. See you soon."

"'Bye." I shut the phone and followed Ellie to the cash register where we completed the transaction.

As I headed out the door laden with the most expensive gown I'd ever seen, I didn't know whether to laugh or cry. All my worrying over Mom and Dad's money had been unnecessary. I'd always assumed they didn't have much money since they were so frugal.

It was with a much lighter heart that I entered my dorm. Money was no longer anywhere on my worry list. All I needed to do was pass my exams and try to look my best on the wedding day. That shouldn't be too hard.

Mom and Dad and all the kids arrived two days before the wedding. They stayed at a hotel close to the Salt Lake Temple. The kids loved the pool.

Mom and Dad seemed to be enjoying the atmosphere. "It's so nice having a maid clean the rooms and make the beds." Mom confessed.

I hid my surprise. Mom had never acted like she minded the menial tasks around the house.

"Where are the kids going to stay while I get my endowments out tomorrow?" I asked.

"Mary's twelve. She's old enough to watch the others for the two-hour session. We'll just come back and get them before we eat dinner."

"I forgot Mary can babysit. Are you sure she'll be okay in a hotel room?"

"Dad's sister, Aunt Tina, and Uncle Brett are arriving in a couple of hours. They'll be in the room next to ours during tomorrow's session. If there's a problem, Mary knows she can contact them. Aunt Clara and Uncle Travis will be here later tonight, as well. Their oldest daughter, Connie, will be watching all the kids in our room during the wedding day after tomorrow. She's a senior this year, so I think she can handle it. Mary's excited to watch Tina's son. Connor is just a couple of weeks old. I'm surprised Tina feels well enough to travel."

"I'm glad they're coming to the wedding. I know Mary is excited to watch Connor. She's always loved babies." I felt a wave of relief wash over me. They weren't my kids, but they were my siblings, and I worried unnecessarily. Mom always made sure we were safe.

After I dressed in white, I followed Mom down the hall to a small room. Mark and his parents were already there. A man whose white hair closely matched his attire discussed the importance of our temple covenants and how we should dress after the endowments were given. As he talked, I reached over to touch Mark's hand.

I almost gasped aloud as I felt a wave of darkness wash over me. I glanced up and wondered if Mark felt it, too. He sensed my gaze focus on him. His gray eyes smiled down at me.

He didn't seem to be feeling the same darkness I felt. *Something must be wrong with me.* I bit my lip then smiled tremulously back at Mark. *I'm the daughter of a rapist. I don't belong here. Who am I to think I belong in this holy place?*

I had to resist the urge to stand up and run out of the room, screaming. *Mom told me the temple was a peaceful place. Why don't I feel peace? I thought evil couldn't enter this holy edifice. I must be carrying something with me.*

I tried to remember my interview with the Bishop. I hadn't felt evil then. I'd been looking forward with joyous anticipation to my trip to the temple.

Maybe I only feel this darkness here because I don't belong here. My creation was a mistake. Mom never meant for me to be born. My birth father was a monster. I shouldn't be here. Once again, I resisted a powerful urge to stand up and leave.

As the endowment session progressed, I became wrapped up in the story and pondered on the session ripe with symbolism. What did it all mean? How did it apply to my own life? What strength could I draw from the words that were being said?

It wasn't until I stood up to pray with Mark that I remembered my earlier feeling. It enveloped me when he touched my hand. The lights in the endowment room flickered.

The Lord doesn't want me here. I shouldn't be here. I'm not worthy to be in this sacred place. Tears coursed down my face.

I was glad everyone's eyes were closed. I could hear other sniffles in the room, so I knew I wasn't the only one moved to tears. My tears weren't like theirs, though. Mine were tears of sorrow. Sorrow that I didn't belong here with everyone else. *My creation was a horrendous mistake. I shouldn't even be alive. Why am I here?*

When I sat down again, a feeling of peace enveloped me. For a moment, I was stunned. *How could my feelings be changing so drastically? What can it mean?* I tried not to think about my feelings and instead concentrated on the oration.

Once again, I was lost in the symbolism of the session. A variation of the Young Women theme whispered in my mind. *I am a daughter of Heavenly Father, who loves me.* A flood of peace enveloped my heart. *I do belong here. This is right.*

As it had just a few weeks earlier, the second Article of Faith crossed my mind. *"We believe that men will be punished for their own sins and not for Adam's transgression."*

In a way I'd never processed before, my mind opened. *How I was created has nothing to do with me. It has to do with my father. I am not responsible for my father's crime. I will not be punished for what he did.*

The peaceful reassurance that I was not responsible for my father's actions stayed with me until Mark touched my hand as we entered the Celestial Room. Once again, a surge of darkness spilled over me. *Satan must not want me to marry Mark. But I didn't think Satan could enter the temple. I don't understand these feelings.*

Later that evening while we were eating dinner with the family at a nearby restaurant, Mom tried to catch my eye. When she did, she whispered, "Christina. You're being awfully quiet. Are you okay?"

"Yes." I toyed with my food a moment. "I'm not very hungry. I think I'll go to the room. May I have the keycard?"

"Certainly." Mom fished through her purse and pulled out the card. "Dad has another key, so you don't need to wait up. I know today's been a big day. Tomorrow's your wedding. You should be rested for the ceremony and the pictures afterword. Mark's family felt the same. That's why they all stayed at a different hotel. They thought you and Mark would get more sleep if you weren't together tonight."

I nodded. I could hardly see my way to the elevator. At least I hadn't started to cry until I left the table. *Must be wedding nerves.* I tried to convince myself, but another thought intruded. *It's bigger than that.*

I clenched my hands into fists until the nails bit painfully into the flesh. *What am I thinking? The wedding is tomorrow. All the families—mine and Mark's—have arrived for the wedding. Most of them flew.*

I tried not to see dollar signs in my head, but they wouldn't go away. The wedding dress alone was a small fortune. Never mind the deposit on the reception hall, the photographer, the flights for everyone, the flowers. I bit my lip.

What are these feelings I'm having? Am I doing the right thing? I remembered Mark's gray eyes smiling down into mine at the temple earlier in the day. I couldn't help but smile in response. I loved Mark with an intensity that scared me.

But the feelings I had in the temple were real. I can't deny it. Is marrying Mark the right thing? I thought back to the time I'd fasted for an answer.

You know you never got your answer. Then I remembered clearly the thought I'd had when I was making out my traits list. *He doesn't love others as himself.* I'd been angry then. I'd thrown the crumpled sheet into the trash. *Maybe I didn't want to hear the answer.* I angrily rolled to my stomach and pulled a pillow over my head, trying to shut out the voice that wouldn't be silenced. *Maybe I don't want to hear it now. It's too late. Too late.*

Those two words were pounding in my aching head when I heard the keycard slot being activated. I pretended to be asleep when Mom, Mary, and Julie entered the room. They must've watched a movie in the next room. It was almost 10:00 p.m. The boys were sleeping in the next room with Dad.

"Shhhh. Christina's asleep. I don't want you to wake her up. Tomorrow is a big day."

Even in my state of extreme turmoil, my lips twitched as Julie nearly shouted, "Okay, Mommy. I'll be quiet, I promise."

"Come into the bathroom to change, please, and you need to whisper, Julie. That means talking quietly."

Julie's loud whisper wasn't much quieter than her earlier voice. "Sorry, Mommy, I forgot."

I remained wrapped up in my blanket cocoon while Mom and my sisters prepared for bed.

Less than half an hour later, deep breathing was emanating from the king-sized bed next to mine. Once they were asleep, my restlessness couldn't be contained. I tossed and turned.

What if I'm making the biggest mistake of my life? The marriage will be a covenant between me, Mark, and God. I can't just walk away from that. Dollar signs flashed in my head. Thousands of them.

What am I going to do? I should've taken more time to make this decision. I can't just call it off now. I would be utterly humiliated. I shuddered.

I don't even want to think how Mark will handle this. His parents flew all his brothers and sisters and their kids from all over the United States. And the wedding breakfast. I'm sure the reservation can't be cancelled now.

The last time I remembered looking at the clock, it was 2:17 a.m. When Mom was singing "Good Morning to You," I looked at the clock. It was 7:30 a.m. *Five hours of sleep. Great.*

I sat up groggily, yawned and stretched.

Mom tilted her head to the side. "Somehow, you don't look like you got enough sleep."

Not wanting her to know how little I had slept, I answered. "It's just wedding jitters. I'm fine."

"Hmm. Well. You'll need a lot of makeup to hide those dark circles." She turned her attention to brushing Julie's hair while addressing me. "Let's eat breakfast. I'll help you with the makeup afterwards."

"Sounds good." I croaked. *Yikes. My voice isn't even working. Super.* I thought with some sarcasm. *Is anything going to go right today?*

Breakfast reminded me of the first meal I'd eaten after I'd fasted about my decision. The food had tasted like sawdust then, too.

After breakfast, Mom worked on my makeup. When she finished, she stepped back to inspect me. "You're beautiful, Honey. Thanks to the modern miracle of makeup, your shadows have disappeared."

My smile was weak but my hug was warm and tight. "Thanks, Mom. I love you. I'm so glad you're here."

Mom's face wore a look of surprise. "Of course, I'm here, Sweetie. I wouldn't miss this for the world." I could see the glint of tears in her eyes. I couldn't imagine how it felt to be marrying off her oldest daughter. Images of all our years together flashed through my mind. With a pang, I thought, *I hope I can always be close to my mom. I don't ever want to lose that, no matter how old I get.*

I was surprised to see five other brides in the bridal dressing room in the temple. I'd honestly believed that no other bride would be getting married so close to Christmas. *I guess I'm not the only crazy one.*

Mom opened up the dress bag and helped me put the gown on. I turned to stare at myself in the mirrors designed to show multiple angles. "Wow. I forgot how much I like this dress."

"You're stunning, Honey. It's a beautiful gown. It brings out your inner beauty."

I tried to force a smile. I wasn't successful. "It should for the amount we paid for it."

"Honey, I told you not to worry. It's a lovely gown, and you don't need to think about any expenses related to the wedding."

I sighed. "I know, Mom...It's just..." and I stopped myself because I didn't know what to say. *I don't dare whisper a word about my cold feet. Doesn't every bride have cold feet? I'm feeling normal wedding jitters, that's all. I don't need to worry my mother.* I hugged Mom and followed her out the door. I was glad she hadn't pressed me to explain.

Mom, Dad, and I entered the sealing room before Mark and his family. I watched as Mom's cousins filed in. Her aunt and uncle were on a mission and hadn't been able to attend. Dad's brother and sisters and his parents found their way into the room and sat down in the cushioned chairs.

When Mark entered followed by his family, my breath caught. *How can this absolutely perfect guy want me?* I shocked myself by remembering I hadn't yet told him about my background. About who my father was. *I haven't been fair to him,* I thought. When he sat down next to me and reached for my hand, I felt black clouds of despair wash over me.

I tried to listen as the sealer gave advice on how to keep the love alive in our marriage. "You might consider murder," he joked and the room filled with quiet snickers, "but never divorce. Let those words not enter your vocabulary." I couldn't hear the rest of his sermon. My mind was in turmoil.

As we made our way to the altar to make our vows, I listened to the words of the sealing prayer. When it was my turn to say "yes," all eyes rested on me.

"No." I could hardly say the word. When the sealer's eyes opened wide with shock, my voice took on conviction and strength. "No." I said again and pushed away from the altar.

Mark's face turned purple with rage. "You...you little tramp. How can you do this to me?" His enraged shout had several guests staring in open amazement.

No one shouts in the temple, I thought.

Somehow, his behavior wasn't a surprise. I suddenly realized our whole relationship had been about him. He hadn't once asked me how I felt about anything. If I felt strongly about something, I'd had to force him to stop and listen. I didn't want to spend my entire life fighting. His apoplectic rage was out of place in the temple, and it would have been out of place in my life.

As Mark continued to spew out his anger, his mother flew to his side. Her face carried the same purple rage, and it was easy to see where he had inherited his temper. Several men in dark suits, ear phones attached to their ears, entered the room and escorted Mark and his enraged mother down the hall.

Mom had rushed to my side and wrapped her arm around me as we faced Mark's angry father. His face hadn't taken on the contortions of Mark and his mother, so I had some hope we could converse with him.

I overheard one of the shocked guest's loud whisper, "I didn't know the temple had security guards."

Honestly, I thought, *I didn't know there was a need for security guards in the temple.*

Dad spoke with the officiator then turned to the assembled group. Calmly, he said, "I know many of you have travelled some distance for this event. We don't want you to have to travel without some sustenance. We'd like to invite you to attend the wedding breakfast as originally planned. The reception later tonight is cancelled." When Mark's dad looked like he wanted to interrupt, Dad held up his hand to stop him and continued, "The breakfast will be hosted by my family."

Mark's father looked relieved at the mention of Dad paying for the event.

I pulled the heavy gold ring from my finger and handed it to Mark's father. When he looked down at it, his mouth started to work on a sentence I didn't want to hear. Mom and I retreated to the dressing room. I had no desire to speak to any of the assembled guests, and I wanted to avoid Mark's family at all cost.

Tears were coursing down my cheeks as Mom helped me step out of my gown. Between sniffles, I mumbled, "Maybe we can get a refund on the dress."

"It's your choice, Honey."

I peeked at her through wet lashes. I couldn't imagine what was going through her mind. *She probably thinks I'm a complete idiot.*

Mom must've seen the warring emotions on my face. She hugged me tightly then stepped back. "You don't need to talk about this if you don't want to, but if you need a listening ear, I'm always here."

"Thanks, Mom." Relief washed over me. I wasn't ready to talk, but someday, I might be.

Chapter 10, Israel

I didn't try to explain why I'd broken off the wedding at the last moment. Mom and Dad seemed to accept Mark's response as evidence that he wouldn't have been an ideal eternal companion.

The dorm was for single women, so I'd had to release my room to another student for the coming semester. Despite the misgivings of my parents, I had chosen to move into the apartment Mark and I had managed to find. After my abrupt cancellation of our wedding, I hadn't expected to hear from Mark. I was right. No phone calls. No visits. No letters. Nothing. It was as if I'd never been an intimate part of his life.

The Provo/Orem area didn't have many rooms available during the school term. I didn't have a lot of choices. Even though I'd planned on taking the winter semester off to adjust to married life, I didn't want to move back home. That was more humiliation than I could stand.

The bridal shop had accepted the wedding dress on consignment. If it sold, my rent would be paid for the next few months. If it didn't sell, I'd have to find a higher paying job. The assistant secretarial position paid minimum wage. I'd have to return to BYU to keep my position there, but I'd been allowed a semester off. I was grateful for the exception they'd granted me.

When I returned to work the day I was supposed to have returned from my Hawaiian honeymoon, Leslie's eyes swept over me. Her voice sounded amused. "Looks like you didn't get much sun, Mrs. Sandstrom."

"Miss Andrews." I corrected her, "and I'd rather not discuss it, if you don't mind."

Leslie's eyes went big, and I could see her bite back her curiosity. I knew I wasn't being fair to her, but I just didn't feel like rehashing the entire ugly event. Besides, I could see the "I told you so" glint in her eye, and I didn't want to hear it.

I marched back to my office and dumped the remains of the last bouquet Mark had given me into the trash. I had no desire to keep a reminder on my desk.

After working four hours in my routine job, I felt some kind of normalcy return. It gave me the ability to tackle a task I'd been too distraught to handle. Gifts and letters from friends, family, and acquaintances that had arrived before the wedding needed some kind of response. I knew I should take care of it myself, but I felt overwhelmed any time I tried to start.

Mom had suggested I return as many items as possible to the stores where they were purchased so I could get the money back. Sending a check was not as expensive as mailing bulky items. I'd already done the returns. I'd spent the week I was supposed to be honeymooning in Hawaii taking care of them.

It was the notes I was dreading. I spent a couple of hours at the kitchen counter writing apology notes. I had one note left.

I sat and stared at a frilly white envelope. It had Nan's familiar neat writing. "Mr. and Mrs. Mark Sandstrom" was written across the front of the card. I hadn't even opened the letter. I turned it around in my hands. I dreaded this note more than all the others.

Slowly, I slit open the envelope. The card had an ink drawing of the Salt Lake Temple on the front. Tucked inside was a check signed by Todd. I was surprised to see water splash on the check and realized it was a tear. I quickly wiped away the next one and tried to read the note handwritten on the inside. It was Nan's writing again. "We wish you the best as you begin another step in your eternal journey." I couldn't help but smile. It was so Nan.

I pondered a moment and wondered what I should say. As I was thinking, I scribbled VOID across the front of the check. Finally, I opened a blank card and wrote:

Dear Nan and Todd:

Thanks for your generous gift. I really appreciate your thinking of me.

I chewed my lip for a moment, trying to think of how I should continue the note. The other notes hadn't required so much thought.

After receiving my endowments, I realized Mark and I weren't meant to be eternal companions. I called off the wedding.

Your friendship meant a lot to me this past semester. I wish you the best in the coming years.

I'm enclosing your voided check.

I debated about asking them to call then decided it was pointless. I'd unknowingly hurt Todd. The last time I saw him was when he stormed out of the room Mark and I had been using for Spanish studies. Nan had hardly talked to me the past few weeks.

I pondered again about how I should close the letter. After staring at the wall and thinking of several different closings, I ended the note.

Sincerely,
Christina

I sighed as I stuffed the check inside the note and sealed the envelope. I couldn't imagine I'd ever see either of them again. That thought twisted my wounded heart.

"Honey, we know this year has been particularly hard on you." Mom paused a moment. I was glad the phone didn't show the warring emotions wash across my face.

I could hear her breath of relief when she heard the wry humor in my voice. "Understatement."

"Your Uncle Brett and Aunt Tina need someone to help take care of little Connor while they're touring Israel." Mom waited again. I could almost see her holding her breath. I knew she didn't want to hurt me. She'd been careful in our conversations since That Day—the one that would define the rest of my life.

My brow furrowed in confusion. I knew Aunt Tina nursed her infants. How was she going to continue to nurse if she was going to leave him behind? "Will I be staying at their house, or do they want me to watch him at my apartment?"

"Actually," Mom drew the word out, as if she was relishing the moment, "they want you to go with them."

"Wow. Israel? I get to go to Israel?"

Mom must've been relieved she hadn't set off a torrent of tears. They'd been awfully close to the surface lately. Mom continued hurriedly. "They leave in a month. Is that enough time for you to get ready?"

"I'll make it work, Mom. I can't wait to go." The enthusiasm drained out of my voice, and I asked, "Are you sure they want me along, or are you setting me up?"

Mom was assuring. "They asked for you specifically. You've always been the one to watch their kids when they travel. Connor is still nursing. Tina doesn't want to leave him behind for three weeks. I'll be watching the older three."

"If you're sure…"

"Absolutely positive."

"What do I need to do to go to Israel?"

"You'll need a passport and a few shots. I'll have Tina send you an email of the requirements. She'll know exactly what you need, and I know she'll be thrilled that you're willing to go. I didn't think it would be a problem since you'd been planning to take the semester off, anyway…" Mom's voice trailed off. I could imagine her eyes going big as she realized she'd mentioned a taboo subject.

The semester off was supposed to be time alone with Mark. I bit my lip, trying to steady its trembling. I never used to be so difficult to talk to.

Once more, I surprised myself at my control. No tears. "You're right. It's not a problem, and what an opportunity! I love you, Mom. Tell Dad 'hi' and kiss all the kids for me, will you?"

She tried to hide her relieved sigh, but my sensitive phone caught it. She continued, "I will, and be looking for that email. It should arrive shortly."

For the first time in several weeks, I was looking forward to the future.

While I was excitedly contemplating my trip to Israel, my phone rang. I glanced at the incoming call. It was the bridal shop.

"Hello? Is this Christina Andrews?"

"It is."

"We found a buyer for your dress, but she wants to pay about $800.00 less than you wanted. Is that acceptable?"

Knowing I would be out of town for several weeks, I was relieved to know I'd have any income from the dress. The amount should cover the rent through the rest of the semester. I felt a sense of relief knowing my room would still be there when I got back. "That's fine. When can I pick up the money?"

"If you're agreeable to the price, she wanted to take it home today. It will take about three days for the credit card to clear. Can you come in then?"

"I can come early in the day. I work in the afternoons. What time do you open?"

"We open at 10:00."

"I'll see you on Friday. Thanks a lot."

"You're welcome. We'll see you then."

I closed the phone with a smile on my face. There was one less worry on my list.

My next worry was Leslie.

She seemed unruffled when I blurted out. "My aunt and uncle are going to tour Israel in three weeks. They'd like me to go with them to watch my nephew. Is there any way I can take a few weeks off?"

"Israel has been closed to travel for some time."

"I know, but the recently-signed peace treaty has opened the borders again. My aunt and uncle want to take a tour while traveling there is allowed."

"I'll talk to the Dean, but I'm sure he'll let you go. The opportunity to see the Holy Land is one you can't pass up."

"I know." I couldn't hide my delighted smile. "Thanks, Leslie."

She nodded then said. "I'll be taking my vacation when you get back from Israel. I'll expect you to fill in for me then."

"No problem." I agreed. I'd been expecting more of a battle. Everything was falling into place. Israel was where I needed to be.

A few weeks later, I met Tina, Brett, and little Connor at the Salt Lake Airport. I recognized them before they had a chance to see me. Tina was about 5'4" with sandy blonde hair. She shared the coloring of my dad. Brett towered above the passengers hurrying to their various destinations. His 6'9" height had assured him a spot on his college basketball team, but he had never been drafted to the pros. He'd chosen a career in real estate instead.

His success paid for their annual two-week break from the kids. I had stayed behind to watch their children often enough that I felt lucky to be included in this one.

Brett's dark hair had begun to show some frost, but he carried his age well. I noticed several attractive women turn their heads as he walked by. Tina didn't even notice as her face lit up to one of his comments. She had nothing to fear.

I hurried over to greet them. "Hi." Their welcoming smiles brought an answering one from me.

Tina reached out and hugged me tight. "We're so glad you decided to join us. We wanted to travel to Israel before the borders are closed again."

I nodded. "Good idea. You never know how long it might be." I scanned the crowd. "It looks like everyone else has the same idea."

Brett's pleasant voice joined in. "We're lucky we found any seats. The flights to Israel are booked solid for the next three months. It was sheer luck that a family had to cancel a planned trip, and we got their seats."

"I'm just grateful you're letting me tag along." I interjected.

Tina was assuring. "We're glad you're willing to come. I was worried we wouldn't be able to find anyone to help with Connor, and we really felt we should make the trip immediately given the volatility in the Middle East."

"Will we have any time in New York?" I asked.

Tina answered, "No. There'll be just enough time for a quick meal in the airport. The airline food isn't very satisfying." She wrinkled her nose in disgust. "We thought we'd catch something in the food court between flights. You'll have to enjoy the view from the plane, I'm afraid."

My face flushed with excitement. "I've never been there. Even a view out the window will be more than I ever imagined I'd get."

Tina laughed. "You need to get out more. You're like a kid in a candy store."

"The drive from Kansas to Utah is as far as I've ever gone. I'm so grateful you're including me."

"Well, we're the ones feeling grateful right now. We wouldn't trust Connor with just anyone, you know."

I could feel a blush spread across my face at her compliment. We were interrupted by the announcement of our boarding numbers.

When we settled into the plane, I was grateful for the window seat. I still hadn't gotten over my fear of takeoffs and landings, but watching the unfolding geography so far below was a fascination.

When we rose above the clouds, I turned my attention to the in-flight magazines. There were some interesting articles, and I loved scanning through the flight catalogs. It was almost as good as going to the mall, only my legs were falling asleep from lack of movement. I tried to stretch without bothering the passenger in front of me then gave up the effort. There wasn't enough room between seats for any kind of stretching exercises. I was already dreading the flight to Israel. The stretch of flight to New York was just a fraction of the time needed to travel across the ocean.

Connor handled the flight to New York better than I'd anticipated. Whenever he got fussy, Tina was able to convince him to nurse. I hoped the stretch to Israel would go just as well.

As the plane approached LaGuardia Airport, I got a quick glimpse of the Statue of Liberty. Her upheld welcoming arm brought tears to my eyes. *So many refugees have seen her welcome. What an honor to be here seeing her standing in the harbor.*

After the plane landed, I stood with the other passengers preparing to depart.

I scanned the other faces with open curiosity. The passengers were from every nationality and creed. Women in traditional Muslim head coverings, some with young children, others wrinkled with age, appeared in rows next to long-bearded men in traditional Jewish clothing. Women with large crucifixes and prayer beads worn around their necks stood next to skimpily clad tourists swaying on their feet, obviously intoxicated.

The flight attendants must've been selling a lot of alcohol. Since we didn't drink, I hadn't been paying attention.

A group of five arguing men stood out. Their features were oriental. I guessed Japanese. Todd would've known what they were saying. I couldn't speak the language. I turned to Brett and whispered. "Didn't you go to Japan on your mission?"

He nodded, his eyes riveted on the loud men.

"What are they shouting about?" Tina asked, her eyes widening in alarm.

"It's been so long since I left my mission, I can't understand it all, but it has something to do with a delivery that needs to be made." A furrow between Brett's brows revealed his concern.

I wrinkled my nose in disgust. "I thought Japanese people were mild and unassuming."

Brett nodded. "They don't think it's polite to draw attention to themselves, but I have a feeling the alcohol consumption destroyed their restraint."

I was relieved when the men stumbled off the plane. We were several rows behind them, so they were out of ear shot when we left the plane.

Tina carried Connor, who was sleeping in a baby sling.

We wandered through the airport until we found a pizza deli. Tina turned to me, her voice enthusiastic, "If you do one thing in New York, you have to try their pizza."

Different slices of pizzas were displayed in a case at the front of the deli. I was adventurous and chose the spinach and ricotta cheese pizza. While we were waiting for the slices to cook, I walked over to the dessert display. Decadent chocolate layered cake slices were displayed next to several varieties of cheese cake, cookies, and a layered dessert. "What's that?" I asked the clerk, who was standing behind the case.

"Baklava." His Italian accent was charming.

"Isn't baklava a Greek dessert?"

"That one is the Turkish version." He smiled. "We aren't prejudice here. We serve anything that tastes good."

I smiled at his enthusiasm. "I haven't ever tried it." I glanced up at Brett. "Do you mind if I order some dessert?" He was footing the bill. I thought I should ask.

"Go ahead, but I have to warn you baklava is very rich. You don't need much."

I looked back at the clerk. "I'll just have one piece, then."

He placed a small slice of baklava on a paper plate and slid it across the counter.

Brett paid for the pizza and desserts while Tina and I found a booth to sit in.

He joined us with a tray full of our water bottles, pizza slices, and desserts.

The spinach and ricotta mixture was different from any other pizza I'd eaten. White sauce topping the bread had a slight garlic flavor. I chewed on the pizza, enjoying the unique blend of flavors. After I finished my pizza and water, I cut a small piece of baklava with a fork.

I stared at the layered sweet for a moment, almost regretting the need to digest such a work of art. *How long did it take to make all those tiny layers?* I wondered.

Tina broke into my thoughts with a giggle. "Aren't you going to eat it?"

"I was just wondering how long it took to make this."

Brett chuckled. "A lot longer than it takes to eat, I hope."

I grinned back at them then inserted the small bite. Honey soaked phylo dough melted in my mouth leaving behind a trace of finely chopped nuts. *Must be walnuts. I can feel my tongue tingle.* I'd always had a slight allergy to walnuts, but I loved the flavor.

"Well?" Brett asked. He was enjoying his own dessert, a slice of cheesecake piled with cherries and drizzled over with a red sauce.

I swallowed the bite. "I can see what you mean about being rich. I'm glad you warned me." I stared down at the remaining baklava sitting on my plate. "I adore the crunchy sweetness. It's not like anything I've ever tasted, but I couldn't possibly eat more than one piece."

Tina nodded. "I love baklava, too, but chocolate has my vote." She was finishing her slice of German chocolate cake. Pecans and coconut were visible in the icing oozing between the layers and flowing over the top of the chocolate cake.

For a brief moment, I envied her choice, but the second bite of baklava wiped out such thoughts. I'd heard someone call baklava the food of the gods. At that moment, I agreed. Baklava was a delight for the senses.

After we finished our meal, we walked back to the waiting plane.

We managed to make it back to our row in the airplane without waking Connor. Brett stepped forward and whispered, "Do you mind if I take the window seat? I think you ladies would have an easier time walking up and down the aisle with Connor if he needs to be walked."

"Good idea," Tina whispered back. I stifled a chuckle. I couldn't imagine Brett's bulk walking up and down the narrow aisle with a fussy baby.

Brett slid between the seats to the window seat. I held the sleeping baby in his car seat while Tina sat down next to Brett to buckle up. She turned to take him from me. Since he was only three months old, I hoped he would sleep through most of the trip. During the flight to New York, Tina's nursing had seemed to sooth him when the air pressure changed.

I'd heard horror stories about infants screaming through hours-long flights. It wasn't something I wanted to live through.

As I pondered the possibility of an hours-long screaming session from my precious nephew, one of the Japanese businessmen stumbled past my seat. The reek of alcohol followed his passage like an invisible banner. My nose wrinkled at the stench. From the sounds coming through the thin bathroom door, it sounded like he was losing his fermented lunch.

I swallowed hard. I didn't think the baklava that had gone down so pleasantly would taste quite the same coming up.

When he emerged from the tiny cubicle, his skin had a definite green undertone. *Ugh. I hope he's not going to spend the entire trip to Israel stumbling up and down the aisle.*

The takeoff was smooth. I didn't even feel the need to grip the armrests. I was beginning to trust that the airplane wouldn't disintegrate just because I happened to be on board.

A few minutes after the seatbelt sign turned off, one of the other Japanese businessmen stumbled his way down the aisle. After his lunch was lost, I grabbed my purse and rushed to the bathroom. My stomach was already on edge from the movement of the plane. The stench and sounds coming from the bathroom tipped the scale.

I was right. Baklava wasn't meant to be eaten twice.

I pulled a small pack of wipes from my purse and began cleaning my face when noticed a smart phone sitting on the shelf above the tiny sink. I stared at it a moment, wondering if I should do anything with it. The plane experienced some turbulence. I ended up launched against the wall while the phone clattered inside the small sink.

It was obvious the phone wasn't going to do well in the bathroom. I picked it up hoping to see who the owner was. The message flashing on the screen looked vaguely familiar. I stared at it a moment and realized it was my own twitter handle. Carpe Diem in Japanese, unless I was reading wrong. But it had the same distinct letters I'd become familiar with. *It must belong to one of those sick guys.*

I couldn't speak their language, but I knew Brett did. *Should I take the phone to him? He'd know how to communicate with them, and I'm not certain it's Japanese, anyway.* I bit my lip in indecision then another turbulent moment threw me into the wall. The phone flew from my grasp as I grabbed the sink for support. The "fasten seatbelt" alarm screamed, almost drowning the sound of the flight attendant telling another passenger just outside the door to take their seat. I grabbed my fallen purse and stuffed the pack of wipes inside, then hurried back to my seat.

Tina looked up in concern as I sat down and slid my purse under the seat in front of me. "Are you alright?"

I tried to smile, but it probably looked like a grimace. "I've been better. The good news is I don't have anything left to lose."

She echoed my grimace. "That bad?"

"I'm afraid so." I answered as I clicked on my seatbelt. I rested my head wearily against the seat. My session in the bathroom had worn me out. Despite the turbulence, I fell asleep within a couple of minutes.

Even though Connor's cry was a tiny infant one, it broke through my dreams. My tired brain took a moment to remember where I was. When my eyes focused, I could see dark outlines of fellow passengers silhouetted by a few small overhead lights above the heads of reading passengers. Some of the surrounding passengers were stirring and glaring at Tina, who was trying to sooth Connor.

Brett glared back. His intimidating size was enough to have them turning around and pretending not to be annoyed. My attention moved to the group of intoxicated businessmen who had been so obnoxious earlier. They slumped in their seats, a couple of them snoring loudly.

It would take a quick plunge in the ocean to wake up the group. I let out a small sigh of relief. I didn't think they would be understanding of Connor's discomfort.

"It's the altitude." Tina whispered. "It hurts his ears."

How can she tell? I wondered. *Must be a Mom thing.* I glanced down at Connor, his face distorted with infant

130

anger. He was waving his fists next to his ears. *Maybe that's the clue. I wouldn't have picked up on it.*

Tina persuaded Connor to take her breast. The ensuing silence was welcome. I looked past Tina and Brett to the window. The black glass reflected the dim lighting of the cabin. There was nothing to see.

After my lengthy nap, I couldn't relax enough to go to sleep.

I flipped through a newspaper I'd bought in New York and stopped at a headline. "Genetically-Modified Organisms Banned in Europe." *Europe has been protesting GMOs for years. This is nothing new, but why is Europe banning them?* I'd always considered GMOs as harmless since all grains had been genetically modified at some time. Modification was part of the domestication process. Everyone knew that. Corn, wheat, oats, they'd all gone through some kind of change over the history of man. *What is the harm?*

As I read the article, I began to see that the problem wasn't so much genetic modification as much as what it was being modified for. The GMOs were largely modified to accommodate wide-spread use of weed killers. Whatever genetic enhancement that prevented the agricultural crop from being adversely affected by the weed killer was allowing the poison to mingle with the plant DNA. When people ate the plant saturated with the poison, severe health problems followed.

I closed the paper and stared blankly at the overhead screen playing a movie I didn't have earphones for. I was remembering the manuscript I'd typed just a couple of months before on the link between fast-rising yeast and celiac disease.

Is the yeast a GMO? If so, what kind of genetic engineering created it? When I read the manuscript I was typing, I wasn't seeing a problem. It was all supposition, but that coupled with this article puts things in a different perspective. What have we done?

I shook my head to clear the jumbled thoughts. *Who am I to concern myself with these things? I'm only one. What can I possibly do? I don't understand any of this, but my gut tells me something is wrong.*

How could wheat make so many people sick when D&C 89 *says clearly that wheat is for the use of man? Something isn't right, and I know the one in the wrong isn't God.*

Chapter 11, Flight

Feeling helpless at addressing the food issue, I read a few more articles before I nodded off again.

I didn't know how long the sun had been up when I woke to the sound of the food cart bumping down the aisle. The flight attendant serving our end of the cabin had just stepped by the Japanese men, who were still passed out. *What kind of beverage can knock someone out for so long?* I wondered. *If we're lucky, they might just stay down for the next few hours.* I shuddered at the thought of them being mobile again. They weren't people I wanted to have any interaction with.

My stomach surprised me with a growl of hunger. *I must be feeling better if my stomach is talking to me.* I smiled wryly. *Face it, your illness was purely psychological.* I couldn't argue with that since I only felt sick after the two Japanese men had emptied out their own stomachs. My stomach churned warningly when I turned to that thought. Ugh.

I stared out the window to distract myself. All I could see was blue sky and a few wispy clouds. I wasn't close enough to the window to see what was below the plane. Brett had the window seat. I suspected all I would see was ocean. Not much of interest there.

The red-headed flight attendant smiled as she greeted me. "Did you want the sausage biscuit sandwich or the egg and cheese?"

"Sausage biscuit. I'd like orange juice to go with it, please."

"Certainly." She looked past me to address Tina and Brett.

Tina's face showed exhaustion. I guessed she was feeling the effects of trying to keep little Connor quiet. *I wonder if she's been up all night?*

"I'd like the same, please, and so would m-my husband." Tina's voice cracked. She reached a hand trembling with exhaustion to sweep hair out of her eyes.

Brett was snoring next to Tina. He wouldn't be stirring any time soon, but I was sure he'd be hungry when he woke up.

I passed the food and beverages to Tina, who placed them on her open tray. When I finished my own breakfast, I folded up the tray then asked, "Would you like me to hold Connor while you eat?"

"Thanks." The intense relief that flooded across her face made me feel guilty that I hadn't offered earlier. *I'm tagging along to help with Connor. I should've held him earlier so Tina could get some sleep.*

The food carts had been put away when Tina picked up her breakfast sandwich. Connor started fussing, so I undid my seatbelt and stood up in the aisle. I hoped the difference in position would help.

As I bounced gently and patted Connor's back, he started to suck his fist and was soon nodding off. Luckily, none of the other passengers needed to make a trip to the bathroom, so I had the aisle to myself.

After Tina finished her breakfast, I asked, "Do you want to sleep for a bit? I think I can handle Connor."

"Are you sure?" She protested, but her desire for sleep showed on her face.

"I'll be fine. I'll wake you if I need something."

"Thanks, Christina. I really appreciate it."

When it seemed as though Connor had finally fallen into a deep sleep, I moved to buckle him in his car seat. Since we weren't changing altitude for a few hours, he would hopefully remain asleep.

I sat back and clicked my own seatbelt in place. I pulled out a notebook I'd stuffed in a side pouch of my purse. *This is as good a time as any to start writing in my journal.* I'd never wanted to write, but Nan's dedication to the cause had inspired me. I was surprised by how easily my life story slid out from under my pen. Connor's quiet fussing a couple of hours later found me with nearly twenty written pages. It was in my large scrawl, but it was all there in black and white. I stretched, happy at my accomplishment then tucked the notepad and pen back in the side pouch so I could pick up Connor.

Tina was still knocked out, but Brett was starting to stir. I stood up with Connor so I could bounce him. Several minutes later, Connor's fussing turned into an enraged howl. Brett's concerned glance caught mine. "We must be changing altitude. He needs to nurse." Brett gently shook Tina.

She moaned, then opened her weary eyes and sighed. "I suppose I need to take Connor again."

"I'm sorry. I can't soothe him." I said.

"Don't worry about it. I'm sure you did your best."

Even as tired as she was, she smiled down at Connor. The adoration in her eyes brought tears to mine. I bit my lip and stared blindly down the aisle. *I might be expecting my own if Mark and I...* I cut the thought off. It was useless to think about what might have been. I knew my decision in the temple had been right, but I was surprised at the intensity of my longing for a child of my own.

I wonder what Todd is doing? The thought surprised me, but thinking of Todd was definitely preferable to the alternative.

As we banked over Tel Aviv to head for the Ben Gurion Airport, I couldn't help the thrill of excitement that ran up my back. *I'll be walking where the Savior walked.*

The businessmen were sitting up groggily and staring around, as if disoriented. I'd never had a hangover, so I had no clue what they were going through. The food carts had been put away in preparation for landing. They were out of luck if they needed some coffee to revive.

One of the men was shuffling through his pockets as if he'd lost something.

The captain's voice sounded over the intercom. "Welcome to Tel Aviv. The ground temperature is 75° F or 24° C with humidity of 70%." *Sounds like Kansas,* I thought as the captain's voice droned on. "Thanks for flying Delta. We hope you enjoyed your flight, and please choose Delta next time you fly."

The flight attendants were walking down the aisle one last time, inspecting the passengers to ensure they were buckled.

I settled back with a sigh. I would be on the ground in Israel in just moments. My skin tingled.

As I stepped out into the bright sunshine, I breathed in the humid air. I had grown accustomed to the dry Utah climate. I could almost feel my skin sucking up the moisture. I wouldn't be needing any lotions here.

Brett's deep voice broke into my thoughts. "Tina and I wanted to stop at the Lod Mosaic Center before we moved on to Jerusalem."

My brow furrowed in question. "What's that?"

"A nearly-perfect floor mosaic was unearthed when Ha-Halutz Street was being widened. It covers about 1,900 square feet and has been dated to the third century. Because it doesn't have any inscriptions, it is assumed the mosaic was from a private residence."

"Wow. That sounds interesting. How far is it?"

"Just a few minutes from here, if we can find a taxi to take us."

Tina, Connor secured in a sling, was standing at the curb waving. A half-full taxi pulled over, but Tina waved them on before Brett joined her. A couple more taxis stopped and left before an empty taxi appeared. "Can you take us to the Lod Mosaic Center?" Brett asked.

The driver nodded. We all climbed into the back while the driver loaded the luggage into the trunk.

As Brett promised, it only took a few minutes to find the center. A description of the mosaic and how it was found was displayed. It was with some fascination I walked through the center and saw first-hand a place where an ancient artifact had been found. In this land, any given spot could harbor any number of finds. *I wonder how many thousands of feet have stood where I am standing and if one of them had personally met Jesus.*

"Next stop, Jerusalem." Brett grinned at Tina.

"Where are we staying?" I asked.

"It's a hotel on King David Street. It's close to the division between the Old City and the new. Most of our tours are within walking distance of the hotel." Brett answered.

"That's convenient." I approved.

Tina nodded. "Since we're leaving Connor with you, I wanted to be close enough so you could call me if you needed something."

"I think I'll be able to handle him, but I'm glad you'll be close, just in case."

We loaded into the waiting taxi and travelled on to Jerusalem. I didn't know what I was expecting, but traffic heavy enough I could step from hood to hood all the way to

Jerusalem was a surprise. I turned to Tina, my brows raised in surprise. "What's up with all this traffic?"

"Since the Israeli boarders have been closed for so long, tourists from all over the world are taking advantage of the opening while they can." Brett answered my question.

"Just like us." I laughed and stared in amazement at the cars, loaded tourist buses, and the variety of trucks hauling goods into the city. "I hope you'll be able to see what you want to see. It might be 'standing-room-only' all over the city."

Tina shuddered. "I hope not. I'm not into close body press crowds." She reached over to touch Brett's hand. "I'm just glad we could come. I've wanted to see Jerusalem for years."

Brett's adoring smile at Tina twisted my heart. *Mark should be looking at me like that right now.* I turned my attention to the crowded road once more. I needed a distraction. *I wonder what Todd is doing? Is he happy?* An image of him tenderly kissing his sister farewell filled my mind.

My brows furrowed as I saw a crowded taxi full of oriental men sway close to my own taxi. The men in the car resembled the men from the flight. Their angry glaring eyes spoke a rage I didn't understand. I shrunk back in my seat and looked away. *What's up with them?* I wondered.

A truck full of produce bore down on the neighboring taxi. I breathed a sigh of relief when the truck replaced the taxi as the neighboring car. The Dome of the Rock appeared, brilliant gold reflecting the evening sun.

Jerusalem. The Holy City. I was on holy ground. I could feel it. Jesus Christ had walked this land.

I wonder if I'll be able to do any sightseeing when Brett and Tina finish their day. I didn't think to ask.

"Doesn't the Dome of the Rock stand right where Solomon's Temple used to stand?" I directed my question at Tina.

"Yes, it does. The Holy of Holies inside the temple is supposed to be there. It is considered the most sacred place in all Judaism. The Muslims believe Mohammed rose to heaven there. When two distinct religions claim the same holy spot, it creates a conflict that can't be resolved. The Temple Mount itself is a constant reminder to all people that the Muslim/Jewish problem is not an easily-solved one."

I glanced out the window, watching the diversity of people traveling toward the city. Softly, I said, "The problem has kept all people out of this Holy City. It's so sad that religious conflict has prevented so many from seeing places of historical significance to many religions."

"Well," Tina interjected while she stroked Connor's dark bit of hair, "I'm just glad the borders have opened at all. With all the conflict here, there's no guarantee the borders will remain open."

Suddenly fearful, I asked, "Do you think it's really safe?" When Tina turned wide eyes to me, I continued, "I mean would they open the borders prematurely to tourists? The country has been hurt by the lack of tourism over the past couple of years. Do you think they'd be hasty?"

Tina chewed worriedly on her lip while Brett answered, "I'm sure the State Department wouldn't put American lives at risk. This is Israel, so there are no guarantees, but I do believe the government felt the signed treaty means the country is safe at the moment." Brett reached for Tina's hand. "I wouldn't risk Tina's life just so we could see the Holy Land."

I breathed a sigh of relief. The taxi full of oriental men had me worried. I stifled a shudder then laughed inwardly.

It's that article I read about the Japanese mafia. I'm seeing things that aren't there.

I tried to figure out the layout of the city, but the maze of streets soon had me hopelessly lost. I was directionally challenged in Utah, famous for its North/South and East/West numbering system. I couldn't hope to stay oriented here. Street names would change from one intersection to the next. *I'm so glad I'm not driving,* I thought in relief. *There is no way I could figure out the layout of the city in the few days we'll spend here.* The Dome of the Rock on top of Temple Mount was an easy way to stay oriented as was the Mount of Olives, but I couldn't always see them from street level.

The driver pulled up in front of an opulent hotel. As I stepped out of the taxi onto the cobbled street, I wondered how many millions of feet had travelled across the spot of land I was touching. A few droplets of water cooled my face from a nearby fountain. I'd heard some of the fountains in the city were hundreds of years old. I wondered if this was one of them.

The very air I breathed seemed heavy with historical significance.

I turned to watch Brett pay the taxi driver then signal for a porter to carry our bags in. Another exchange of bills saw us into our rooms.

"The rooms are connecting." Brett said as he opened a door. "Your room is through the door to the left of this one, but we can go back and forth between rooms without entering the hallway." He raised his brows in question as he looked down at me. "I hope you don't mind. Tina and I thought it would work out better so we could keep Connor's crib in our room. When we're out sightseeing, you can just open the dividing door."

"What a good idea." I smiled in delight.

As I followed Tina into their room, I turned to view the surroundings. The elegant bed and armoire looked as if they had been standing there since the Crusades.

The small crib stationed next to the king-size bed was a more modern design. Connor had slept in a similar folding bed in the days before the non-wedding. I controlled a shudder at the thought. I didn't want to remember anything about that awful day, and I certainly didn't want Tina and Brett to think I was dwelling on the past.

The floors were made of ceramic tile and covered with what looked like hand-made rugs. The colors were vibrant. When I stepped across to the door that joined our two rooms, my feet sunk into the wool. I wanted to strip my shoes off so I could feel the fibers under my toes. *What a silly thought.* I bit my lip on a laugh.

My room was a mirror replica of the one shared by Tina and Brett. I walked over to the window and pulled open the heavy drapes. My eyes widened in surprise at the spectacular view offered on the sixth floor. Jerusalem spread out in all its splendor before me. The city was teeming with people. Even with the mass of humanity, I longed to step outside and feel the dirt under my feet. Dirt that might have been trod by the Savior. No other place on earth could replicate the feeling of Jerusalem.

Tina moved to join me and shared my vision of the Holy City for a few quiet moments. Her soft voice broke into my thoughts. "We thought we'd just order room service for tonight. Do you want to look over the menu and decide what you want for dinner?"

Obediently, I stepped over to the table where the menu sat. I tried to decipher the different dishes. I wasn't familiar with any of them. Finally, I turned to Tina. "What do you recommend?"

"This is our first visit to Israel, so I'm as new at this as you are." She paused and scanned the menu. "I'd guess you can't go wrong with one of the chicken dishes."

"Good idea." I smiled at Tina then continued to peruse the menu. There were five different chicken entrees. I finally picked one that looked vaguely familiar.

The meal was delivered within half an hour. When the food arrived, Tina suggested, "If we all split meals, we can try different flavors and see which one we like best."

"Good idea." I agreed.

Brett divided each of the main entrees into thirds and I obediently took a portion of each of their entrees while they took from my entrée. "What a fun way to experience Israeli food!" I enthused.

After finishing our meals and placing the trays with the plates stacked on them just outside the door, we turned to unpacking. It only took a few minutes for me to unpack my meager wardrobe. I hadn't planned on spending much time on anything but watching Connor, but seeing my pitifully small wardrobe hanging in the immense wardrobe had me wondering if I'd been wise. *I might need something more exciting than jeans and t-shirts.* I mused. I chuckled. *I don't think Connor will really care what I'm wearing when I change his diapers.*

After I unpacked my things, I stepped through the adjoining door. "Did you need help unpacking Connor's stuff?" I directed my question to Tina.

"Sure. His things can be put in the dresser."

As I was unpacking Connor's suitcase, I pulled out a portable DVD player, still in its box. I stared at the wire wrapped around the cardboard box. It almost looked like a four-legged octopus hugging the contents. "How come the alarm is still on the box?"

Tina's eyes widened in horror. "The store must've forgotten to take it off. I didn't notice when I packed."

Change of Heart

"I know how loud these can be. There was one left on a game console we bought last year for Christmas. We couldn't get it off the package. When Dad finally cut the alarm wire, we had to stuff the alarm under a pile of towels until the battery ran out." I shuddered. "I don't think you want to do that here. It was loud enough to wake the dead. The noise would have every police officer in the city pounding on our doorstep."

Tina's bottom lip pushed out in a pout. "I thought I had everything planned out so well. That bites. You were supposed to enjoy the day tomorrow watching movies while Brett and I tour the town."

"It's okay, Tina. I brought my ebook reader. It has several books I haven't read yet. Don't worry about it."

She sighed. "I can't ever go on a trip without forgetting something."

Brett chuckled. "If forgetting to take the alarm off the DVD box is the only thing you forgot, I'll call myself a lucky man."

Tina wrinkled her nose at him. "You'd better call yourself lucky, anyway."

Brett's expression changed as he looked down at Tina. I figured it was time for me to make myself scarce. "What time do you want me in the morning?" I asked.

Tina seemed as absorbed in her silent discussion with Brett as he was, but she managed to answer. "We'd like to have breakfast at eight, but you don't need to get up. We'll leave the adjoining door open so you can hear Connor."

"Okay. Thanks. Sleep well." I scurried into my room and shut the door with a soft click. I knew when I wasn't welcome.

I stepped over to the open curtains and closed them with an audible swish. The emptiness in my heart brought a lump to my throat. *I know I made the right decision about Mark. Why does it hurt so much?*

*Roseanne Evans Wilkins*

I quickly showered and readied myself for bed. A flying leap landed me dead center in the soft mattress. I collapsed back into the bed, my arms spread wide. *I am in the Holy City.* Goosebumps once again ran up my arms. The memory of my painful parting with Mark soon faded into the background as I reviewed my agenda for the following day. The agenda didn't include time for regrets. I only had a few days in Jerusalem. I wanted them packed with memories. Memories that didn't include one moment wasted on Mark Sandstrom. *Todd is here. In Israel.* The thought spoke peace to my soul. *If only he knew how often he fills my thoughts...*

144

Chapter 12, Alarms

I awoke to the sounds of Connor stirring in the next room. He was just starting to emit the soft cry of a three-month old when I tumbled out of bed and crossed the room. The thick rugs felt just as wonderful on my bare feet as I'd imagined they would.

I picked up Connor and smiled down at his little face. How could I not adore this tiny infant?

I coaxed him into taking a bottle. As he was contentedly sucking, I stared out the window. I couldn't see anything but blue sky from where I was sitting. *I wonder where Brett and Tina went today.*

After Connor finished the bottle and he was burped, I walked over to the antique desk sitting against the far wall. Tina had left their itinerary sitting where I could see it. It looked like they planned to be out until 4:00 p.m. *I'm so glad Connor took the bottle. This would have been an impossibly-long day had he refused it.*

Even though he was so young, Tina had left a reader for him. Tina had told me Connor liked the Winnie the Pooh series. I selected the read-alone option and watched Connor perk up at the familiar voices. He babbled and waved his arms. I played the book through again while I ordered my breakfast.

The biscuits were still steaming, fresh from the oven. Strawberry preserves were in a separate bowl. A peak of snow-white whipped cream topped a cup of hot chocolate. I worked slowly through my breakfast, savoring the different flavors. By the time I finished, Connor was sleeping soundly. His full belly and the sound of Winnie the Pooh had lulled him to sleep.

I wandered around the room, admiring the antiques and reveling in the feel of the thick rugs under my bare feet. I stood at the window several minutes watching the stream of tiny people six stories below moving through the streets. Prominent awnings hid the crowds as they passed beneath them. I yearned to be down in the streets mingling with those who were walking on streets Christ himself might have walked.

I sighed then picked up my reader. A leather chair next to Connor's crib looked inviting. I settled in for a good read.

A couple of hours later, Connor's fussing pulled me out of the story. I placed the reader on the table next to the chair then moved to take care of Connor. After he was changed, fed, and burped, I read a couple of picture books loaded on his reader then turned the Winnie the Pooh book on again. I settled him in his car seat so he could sit up and observe the world while I ordered room service.

Whoever delivered the meal would need a tip. I grabbed my purse and scrambled through its contents to find the money. After I found it, I slid the purse under Connor's crib. *Out of temptation's way,* I thought, then wrinkled my nose. *Not like the hotel help is likely to attack me for my purse, still...better safe...*

My lunch was delivered about twenty minutes later. As I handed over the money, I was relieved to see his gratified smile. I wasn't sure what the exchange rate was. I seemed to have handed over an adequate amount.

I picked up the red apple sitting next to my sandwich of cold cuts and bit into the crisp flesh. It tasted deliciously sweet. I closed my eyes to savor the flavor. *I wonder where this apple was grown?* I couldn't remember if Israel even had apple orchards, but it tasted like it had just been picked.

After I finished the apple, I pulled the sandwich apart and ate the meat, cheese, and bread as separate pieces. The soft fragrant bread tasted as fresh as the apple. I marveled at the flavor. I couldn't remember if there was an on-site bakery, but the bread must've been made that morning.

After I finished eating my lunch, I slid the tray and dishes out the door so the maid could pick them up. Connor was still staring around the room with some interest while I ran to the bathroom to change out of my pajamas. I didn't want Tina and Brett to find me still undressed when they returned from sightseeing.

I pulled on a comfortable pair of jeans and my favorite t-shirt. After I'd dressed and brushed my teeth, I moved to the bedroom where the armoire held my few shoes. They stared back at me in neatly ordered pairs. I reached for the running shoes then switched to the sunny yellow sandals that matched my shirt. *I doubt I'll be going far. The sandals will be good enough.*

Around two, I fed and burped Connor then put him in the portable crib for an afternoon nap.

I was absorbed in my book when I heard a slight sound from the adjoining room. Glancing up, I stared at the door between our rooms. My brow furrowed. *Am I hearing things?*

I stared in horror while I watched the connecting door slowly open. A stealthy, dark-haired stranger moved into the room.

I wasn't in track for nothing, ran through my mind as I lowered my head and rammed into the shocked stranger, forcing him back and down into the adjoining room. I quickly stepped back, slammed the door, and turned the bolt.

I rushed back into the room and frantically searched for some kind of alarm to pull. I couldn't see anything, so I grabbed the still-boxed DVD player Tina and I had laughed about just yesterday. A pair of fingernail clippers were sitting on the bathroom counter. They worked for snipping the wire. I wanted to put my hands over my ears to drown out the screaming alarm but grabbed the phone instead. I dialed zero for the hotel front desk and yelled into the phone. "Someone tried to break into my room." All I could hear in response was some kind of foreign babble. *Great. I get the only clerk in the city who can't speak English.*

I'd never taken Hebrew. Spanish wasn't anything like it. Frustrated and desperate, I stood over Connor's crib and wondered what more I could do. *I don't feel safe running down the hallway with the baby. What if there's more than one?* Connor was starting to stir, his deep sleep disturbed by the loud alarm.

I turned as I heard the splintering of the door. The stranger I'd knocked to the floor just a couple of minutes before was facing me. I backed toward the hallway door across the room, hoping the intruder would follow me and leave Connor alone.

Something glinted in the artificial light. A gun aimed at me. The bluish steel flashed. "Oh, no, you don't." I managed through gritted teeth as I grabbed the gun. I'd wrestled plenty of toys from determined toddlers. I doubted his grip was any stronger than theirs. I was right. I felt his grip slip as his eyes widened in surprise. The sliding gun rattled across the floor and hit the door with a loud crack.

He tackled me then, my face smashing into the side of the reader I'd played for Connor earlier that day. Pooh's singsong and Eeyore's gloomy voices were a stark contrast to my pain. My hands were jerked back, and I could hear the snick of handcuffs. The metal was painfully tight.

Even through the alarm, the sound of the key card lock being activated alerted the intruder to a looming interruption. He threw me over his shoulder then rushed through the splintered door, dropping me unceremoniously on the floor as he threw open the window. He pushed out the screen and leaned far out, his head moving back and forth as if he were looking for some means of escape. We were on the top floor. There was no escape.

My eyes grew wide and I started a piercing scream. No way was I going out that window.

His furious slap echoed through the room. "Shut up!" he hissed.

The painful shock took my breath away. I'd never been slapped.

Someone was rushing in the room. I could hear Tina's voice above the screaming alarm. "Connor, Sweetie, are you okay?"

With Brett and Tina distracted by their screaming son, the intruder shoved me out the window and onto a narrow ledge.

For the first time in my life, my voicebox wouldn't work. I had never been scared of heights, but being shoved onto a narrow ledge outside my room had me frozen in terror. One false move and I was dead.

If I somehow managed to stand, I couldn't keep my balance with my hands cuffed behind my back.

My eyes were wide with terror as I stared at my captor. His eyes were narrow slits, and I could see it wouldn't take much for me to convince him to shove me off the edge. I was already on my back, my arms at an agonizingly awkward angle.

I didn't dare make a sound. He stealthily lowered the window then dropped to the ledge beside me. The eight-inch decorative lip effectively hid our presence from the streets below. He pressed himself against the wall and motioned me to silence. I listened in terror as I heard muffled voices sounding from behind the closed window. How could I alert them to my presence without forcing the hand of my captor?

I hadn't ever known how much I valued my life. At that moment, I would give anything to be safely back home in the loving arms of my family. Not even here, on this ledge, so close to my own death, did I wish myself back with Mark. His hold on me was gone.

Footfalls approached the window. *Look down. Look at me.* I silently screamed. *If you just open the window, you'll see me.* It was never opened. *They must think no one is crazy enough to go through the window with a captive in tow.*

I glanced furtively at my captor. His angry sneer stared back at me. *Whoever he is, he is definitely crazy.* My heart beat a loud rhythm in my ears. I was just a hair's breadth away from death, and we both knew it.

Chapter 13, Change of Heart

I don't know how long it took for all the movement in the room beyond the window to die down. I do know that the sun had made his trip across the sky and the moon was well on her way to following suit.

My arms and legs were cramping from the forced inactivity. I yearned for movement, but I was terrified any slight move would plunge me to the street below.

My kidnapper—I had come to think of him as Demon—had remained as still at his post as I was on mine. Other than occasional shifting to move cramped muscles, stretching out his arms and flexing his fingers, he was silent and motionless.

What kind of training enables someone to remain still for hours? I wondered. *What does he want from me, anyway?* I tried to study his face when he wasn't looking at me. It had definite Japanese features, and all the articles I'd read about the Japanese Mafia in Israel screamed at me. *What would the Mafia want from an American citizen? Surely they wouldn't want the involvement of the United States.* Then a thought chilled me. *How would he even know I'm an American? It's not like I posted my passport on the door. Has he mistaken me for someone else?*

Troubled thoughts swirled as my muscles screamed from their forced non-movement. I had locked myself in place from fear that any movement would mean a deadly fall.

As the darkness of deep night enveloped us, my captor must've decided the room behind the window was safe. He carefully reached for the window and pulled it open then crawled inside. I debated whether or not to scream, but I was terrified a deep breath would dislodge me from the ledge.

Demon swiftly twisted my long hair around his fist and grabbed a fistful of my t-shirt with his other hand. He jerked me unceremoniously through the open window. I could feel the window ledge scrape against my skin. As my body hit the floor, I closed my eyes in relief.

The past terrifying hours were forever burned into my consciousness. Circulation in my hands returned with excruciating pain, but I didn't dare utter a sound as tears streamed down my face. Tears of gratitude that I was still alive. Tears of terror because I didn't know yet what Demon had in mind. Tears of pain from the circulation returning to my dead limbs.

He moved stealthily to the hallway door. No sounds were coming from the adjoining room. I couldn't imagine that Brett and Tina would've remained in a room that had proven to be unsafe. *Where are they now?* I wondered. *The American Embassy?*

Demon stuck his head out the door and looked right then left. He grabbed me and hustled me down the hall to the elevator. I debated once more about screaming, but I valued my life. Screaming would surely end it. Besides, I wasn't sure my voicebox would work properly. I could hardly breathe because of my terror.

We rode the elevator down in silence. He moved over and grabbed my arms roughly. I heard a click of the handcuffs. Suddenly, I found my right hand free with the left tethered to my captor. I surreptitiously clenched and unclenched my free fist, wondering how I could possibly escape.

Demon held a cell phone to his ear. He was hissing in an unfamiliar language.

I started to shake, and my teeth chattered. The fear and tension had taken its toll. He glared at me while he continued his conversation. I tried desperately to control my shaking, but it wasn't something I could control.

I stumbled behind him through a brightly-lit corridor. *Shouldn't there be guards here? Where are the police?* Thoughts swirled through my head.

Our handcuff connection was painfully tight. I prayed fervently for help, but no one appeared. *Why doesn't God answer my prayers?* I wondered in anguish. *Please, help me.* I begged.

We stepped out into the brightly-lit courtyard and hurried over to a waiting car. I glanced around, thinking *Why isn't anyone seeing this? We aren't in a dark alley. We're in front of the hotel. Someone, anyone, rescue me, please.*

Demon shoved me ahead of him, the angle awkward with our connection. I stayed on the floor while he slid across the seat. He glared at me and shoved my head down. His meaning was clear. He didn't want me on the seat next to him.

My shivering continued as tears coursed down my face. I tried to form some coherent ideas on how to escape, but my stress level prevented me from thinking clearly. I couldn't process what was going on.

My mouth was a dry desert. I hadn't had anything to drink since I'd had water with my lunch. My stomach gurgled from lack of food. I scrunched down further on the floor, clutching my free arm around my stomach, attempting to hide the sounds of my discomfort. I also desperately needed a bathroom break. My combined pain engulfed me.

I glanced up at the man whose arm was cuffed to mine. Surely he was feeling the same discomforts I was. I noticed a slight strain around his eyes. Hopeful that his needs would prompt him to allow me to take care of my own, I waited in silence. The left side of my face throbbed where he'd slapped me earlier. I didn't want to look at myself. It wasn't going to be pretty.

After several slow minutes, the car stopped. The two people in the front and Demon, dragging me with him, moved stealthily to what looked like an apartment door. Adobe walls towered above us. We quickly entered the building and the door shut with a solid thud. It didn't sound like the kind of door I could kick through with my flimsy sandals.

The men, all with oriental features, argued in hisses for a moment then I was released from the handcuff that had been biting into my flesh. I rubbed my tender wrist and fearfully watched the men.

I had no idea what they had in mind. If they were the Japanese Mafia as I feared, they had a reputation of running sex slave operations in addition to their gun running. I tried to hide my shudder. I always thought I'd rather be dead than allow myself to be raped, but seeing death stare me in the face made me realize I desperately wanted to live.

One of the men shoved me against a wall and said, "Stay thel." Demon pulled out the phone he'd been using earlier and snapped a couple of pictures. I wasn't asked to smile. I wasn't going to.

After the pictures were taken, Demon disappeared into another room. After a moment, he shoved me into the room he'd just vacated.

To my immense relief, it was a bathroom. At least one of my agonizing pains would end. After I took care of my needs, I rinsed my hands in the sink. There wasn't any soap in the filthy room, so I did the best I could to splash clean.

Despite the filth, my mouth was a raging fire. I cupped my hands and sipped the precious water.

After I had quenched my thirst, I stopped and stared at my reflection. A purple welt marred my face, and my eye was almost shut.

Despite my hazardous circumstances, my lips twitched. My brothers would have been proud. The black eye was a doozy. I covered my mouth with my hands as hysterical laughter threatened to burst out. Tears soon followed. I was a mess.

Having two of my needs met meant the other pain loomed larger. I hadn't eaten for hours. My stomach growled in protest. I tried not to think about the sweet crunchy apple I'd enjoyed at lunch time. The harder I tried not to think about it, the more it filled my mind.

I needed to get the image out of my mind. It wasn't helping my hunger.

The closed toilet offered an uncomfortable perch, but it was the only option other than the filthy floor. I sat on the edge of the seat and assessed my situation. It was looking hopeless. The room was windowless. There was no escape there. With three men sitting outside the door, I certainly wasn't getting out that direction. Even if I did somehow manage to escape, where would I go to be safe? *Is there any safe place in Jerusalem?* Suddenly, I remembered the Jerusalem Center. *I know I'd be safe there, but how can I find my way through the maze of streets?*

I couldn't bring myself to kneel on the floor. I opened my heart in pleadings to the Lord. He was my only hope.

After what seemed like hours, my prayer changed to one of gratitude. I didn't think I'd ever find myself in such a hopeless situation and be grateful, but I was alive. I could so easily be dead. I thanked the Lord for preserving my life. With the change of heart came a peace I wouldn't have known. The only hope I had was the Lord. Whatever happened, I would accept the Lord's will.

I stood up and roamed around the small room, looking in the cupboard under the sink. There were a couple of rolls of sandpaper-like toilet paper, an old box of white powder, and a dried-out dirty sponge. I sniffed the powder curiously. It smelled vaguely familiar. I sniffed again. *Baking soda? What's baking soda doing in a bathroom?* Then I remembered it could be used to absorb odors...and it could be used for cleaning.

I sprinkled the powder inside the sink and added some water to make a paste. A few minutes later, the porcelain sink was sparkling white. Somehow, the act of cleaning out the sink gave me some hope. I might not be able to change everything, but I could improve the spot I was in. Having the sink clean helped my spirits rise. *I wonder what Todd is doing? He doesn't even know I'm here.*

I swallowed a lump and studied the dirty floor. Maybe if it was clean, I wouldn't mind laying on it. I worked on my hands and knees with the sponge and the powder until the tile floor was as clean as the sink. I didn't have the energy to work on the toilet. Besides, I doubted baking soda killed germs. I really didn't want to clean a toilet with my bare hands.

I didn't know how long I'd been shut in the small room, but I knew I'd been stuck on the ledge outside the window for hours. I was exhausted. I pulled out one of the rolls of toilet paper to use as a makeshift pillow on the hard tile. The floor could have been a soft mattress. Todd's twinkling brown eyes were the last thing I remembered before sleep overcame me.

Chapter 14, The Note

Todd

"I'll miss you, Todd. Are you sure you can't stay through the winter semester?" Nan asked, tears glistening in her eyes.

I hugged my sister. "I promised Mother and Father I'd help them out. We'll all be back in the spring for my graduation ceremony."

A tear overflowed. It left a wet track down the side of her face. I reached out to wipe it off while she sniffed. "I know. I'm just going to be lonely with you gone."

"You'll have your new roommate."

She snorted. "My experience with the last one wasn't exactly delightful."

I tried to hide the pain that ripped through me. Nan knew me too well. She reached up to touch my face. "I'm sorry I said that, Todd. Please forgive me."

My voice was hoarse with emotion. "There is nothing to forgive." I turned and headed into the glass doors that lead to the Salt Lake Airport terminal. There was no going back. There wasn't anything in Provo for me.

The flight to Tel Aviv was a blur. Between fitful attempts at sleeping, my mind was full of Christina. I had tried to overcome my attraction to her by dating women in my single's ward. It hadn't been successful.

The first time I'd seen Christina was in a black and white picture in Nan's dormitory packet. Her eyes were unforgettable. They stared back at me from the picture as if she could see into my soul.

I had been anxious to meet the person who owned such speaking eyes. I recognized her immediately when she was purchasing her books at the BYU bookstore. I felt it was fate when her book landed on top of my own smaller stack.

I stared out the window on the plane and tried to forget why I hurt so much. Seeing Christina in Mark's arms when I longed to have her in my own had broken something inside me. I didn't even know myself any more.

It was raining when I stepped out of the terminal in Tel Aviv. The rain beat a solemn rhythm that matched my gray mood.

It was New Year's Eve in the United States. Nan and I had shared a quiet Christmas together before I flew back to Israel. The country of my birth hardly noticed the holiday. We celebrated a different new year here. Rosh Hashanah. I tried unsuccessfully to push the celebration with Christina out of my mind. We'd laughed over apple slices and honey in an office perfumed with flowers I suspected came from Mark. The man who now held her in his arms.

I clenched my fists to stifle the pain, then raised my arm in recognition when my mother's black sedan pulled up to the curb. The window rolled down to reveal her youthful face. I bent down to greet her. "Hello, Mother. Thanks for picking me up."

"You're welcome. How have you been?"

I tried to smile, but the corners of my mouth barely turned up. "I've been better." I paused to compose myself. "How have you and Father been?" I asked as I opened the back door and stuffed in the couple of bags I had with me.

"We're heading into the busy season, so things are hectic at home. I hope you're prepared for a major workload."

This time, I chuckled. "Same as always, Mother. Same as always." I shut the back door, then opened the front and sat down in the passenger seat. The door shut automatically.

We were both quiet then. Mother had never been one to talk much. Nan was like my mother that way.

Our home sat on the outskirts of Jerusalem, a section of modern homes designed to mimic the old quarters. When I stepped through the front door, my father met me with a warm hug. "Welcome home, Son. I've missed you."

I smiled at his greeting. "Thanks. I've missed you, too. Nan said to say 'hi' and to let you know she's missing you."

A shadow crossed his face. "I miss my little Nan, but BYU is very good for her."

I agreed. "It is. She has been doing well in her studies."

He nodded. "Yes, she has. We received her grade report just this morning."

Mother interjected. "I never doubted that she would do well. Our little Nan is a hard worker."

"As is Todd." Father added.

"Naturally." Mother's voice sounded preoccupied as she headed into the kitchen. "Todd, can you set the table while I finish preparing dinner?"

"Of course, Mother. Is there anything else I can do for you?"

She was pulling out a prepared green salad from the fridge as she spoke. "No. Everything else is almost ready. The chicken will be done in about five minutes."

Father, Mother, and I sat around the small table a few minutes later. The fragrance from the chicken reminded me how hungry I was. As I started to eat, Mother asked, "Did you find anyone… interesting…this past semester?"

"If you're talking about a girl, no, I didn't."

Mother sighed heavily. "You're not getting any younger, Todd. I was hoping this semester would be better than the past ones."

My crumpled napkin showed my agitation. "Mother, I think I can take care of my own love life. You don't need to worry."

Father's placating voice took over. "Your mother wasn't meaning to pry, Son. We're just concerned about your future. We know you're capable of handling it yourself."

"Thanks." I allowed a small smile to play over my lips. We ate in silence the rest of the meal. After I finished, I carefully stacked my dinner plate and flatware and placed them in the sink.

The quiet sanctuary of my bedroom called to me. Its walls had been absorbing my worries as long as I could remember. Christina wasn't a problem I wanted my parents involved in. I strode down the hall, my bags in my hands. My parents' concerned gaze bore into my back.

The next few weeks found me involved in several audits. Mother hadn't been exaggerating when she said we were busy. I'd go to bed exhausted at the end of every weekday. I'd never been so grateful for the Jewish Sabbath. The entire country shut down. I needed the day off to recover from the rest of the week.

The last Monday in February found me somberly contemplating my future over a slice of cold toast.

"Todd," Father interrupted my heavy thoughts.

I swallowed then asked, "Yes?"

"Mother and I are concerned. Are we working you too hard?"

My brows drew together in confusion. "No." I stared at him a moment. "Why do you ask?"

Father cleared his throat nervously. "You haven't been yourself. You rarely say a word. You spend all your spare time locked in your room." He glanced pointedly at the toast. "You hardly eat enough to keep yourself alive. We are worried."

I stared at the table, trying to untangle my thoughts. If my parents had noticed, things must be worse than I imagined.

I thought Christina's rapid engagement had killed my desire for her, but the pain of her leaving hadn't diminished. If anything, my pain had increased over the past several weeks. At odd times during the day, an image of Christina and Mark together would torture me. Finally, I responded, "I have some things on my mind. It has nothing to do with the workload."

"Is there anything I can do to help?" I could hear the concern in Father's voice.

I sighed heavily. "No, Father. There isn't anything you can do." I decisively slid my chair away from the table and ended the conversation. "There isn't anything anyone can do."

While I was in my office filing the final work of the day, Mother approached me. The worry on her face drew a furrow between my own brows. It wasn't often I saw that look on her face. She handed me a small white envelope.

"Nan sent you this. It's a note from Christina." From the look on Mother's face, Nan must've told her what the note could mean for me. Unless I'd been talking in my sleep, the name 'Christina' hadn't passed my lips since entering Israel.

I reached for the envelope, dreading what the note contained but strangely unable to toss it without reading the contents. Strong mixed emotions flitted across my face. Mother's face reflected the struggle she was seeing in mine.

The pain I'd tried to suppress ravaged me. I couldn't understand why I would feel that way. It wasn't like Christina and I had spent much time together. She'd dismissed our time as if it had been shared between siblings. That wasn't at all how I had felt.

Reluctantly, I opened the note. It took a moment for me to focus. *Her hand wrote this.* I shut my eyes for a brief moment, envisioning her hand caressing the paper as the pen she held glided across the page.

Aware that Mother was watching, I opened my eyes to decipher the elegant script.

Dear Nan and Todd:

Thanks for your generous gift.

I closed my eyes and swallowed as I read that line. The check for her gift had been one of the hardest things I'd ever written. I opened my eyes to continue reading the note.

I really appreciate your thinking of me.

I had to restrain myself from ripping up the note. How many times I had thought of her. She didn't know what she was writing.

After receiving my endowments, I realized Mark and I weren't meant to be eternal companions. I called off the wedding.

The card dropped from my lifeless fingers. I stared at Mother, my eyes wide with shock. Hoarsely, I whispered, "What am I supposed to do with this information?"

Mother stepped over to give me a comforting hug. "I don't know, Todd. I just don't know."

She reached up to touch my cheek. "I don't have any answers, but I know from Nan how much you cared for this girl." She bit her lip, indecision flickering across her face. "If you feel the need to go back to the States, Father and I can handle the extra workload."

I walked across the office and stared out the window at the busy streets below. My hand gripped the heavy open drapery. I suddenly realized my clenching hand was threatening to pull down the curtain rod and released my hold. I turned back to Mother.

"I don't even know how to reach her." My voice was a cry of anguish. "She moved out of the dorms. Christina had told Nan she was going to take the semester off. I deleted her number from my cell phone when she promised to marry Mark." The image of Mark's lips tracing a fiery line of kisses down Christina's throat burned my mind.

I remembered how I'd stomped into the nearest study room and deleted her number from my phone with fingers shaking with rage. I had been appalled that Christina would agree to an eternal commitment from someone she'd only known for a month. My plan had been to woo her through the entire year and then...I swallowed a lump as the unfamiliar taste of tears threatened to overpower me...I'd had every intention of proposing.

Father looked up from the evening news as Mother and I stepped into his den. He must've seen the pain in my face because he muted the television and stood to greet us. "Son, what's wrong?"

My attention was diverted to the screen where I saw something that froze me in place. "Turn it up."

Father stared at me like I'd lost my mind. Again, I insisted, "Turn it up."

He responded to the urgency in my voice and clicked off the mute. The voice of a commentator rang through the room. It was the tail end of a report. "...demanding the return of an item stolen two days ago from Delta Flight 1415 between the United States and Israel. If demands are not met within 72 hours, they will not guarantee the safety of Ms. Andrews." A picture of Christina's distorted face, her right eye swollen and the same side purple with bruising sickened me.

The commentator droned on about the next item of business. Even though Christina's picture was no longer on the screen, I continued to stare, my eyes wide with horror.

Mother was shaking me. "Todd. Todd. TODD. Are you all right?"

I collapsed onto the couch, my head in my hands. Father stepped over and put an arm on my shoulder. "Son, what is it?"

"That. Was. Christina. Andrews."

Father stared at me, a confused expression on his face. Finally, he asked, "Who is Christina Andrews?"

My head was back in my hands. I couldn't respond.

Mother's quiet voice rang out in the silence. "Christina is Nan's old roommate."

"Oh." Father's monosyllabic reply spoke volumes.

I looked up at him then. "What can I do?"

Father had never once seemed to share the beliefs of my mother. Mother had raised us in a faith she had wholeheartedly accepted, but Father had never converted. He had taught us the Jewish practices of his forefathers. Mother had woven the Jewish practices into the LDS faith in such a way that I often had difficulties distinguishing the two ideologies. At that moment when I needed him the most, my Father said, "Let us pray for an answer. God will know how to help us."

All the doubts I carried at his relationship with God melted away. My Father believed in a living God who cared about us. The thought dried my tears and I stared at Father in wonder. How had I never seen this in him before?

We knelt at the couch. My Father offered a simple prayer of supplication. "Dear God. My son spent two of his precious young adult years serving you. Please listen to our pleas and guide him to know how to handle this tragedy. Amen."

It wasn't a prayer that I would offer myself, but it was heartfelt and sincere. If there was any prayer on earth that would be answered, I was sure it would be that one.

I stood up then helped my parents off the floor. I hugged Mother. We both had tear tracks running down our faces. I turned to Father and wrapped him in a warm hug. My hoarse voice could hardly speak. "Thanks, Father." I stepped back and wiped a tear from my eye. I tried to smile in a face full of agony. "I love you." With that, I strode to my room. I needed time to think.

My window overlooked Jerusalem. The evening hadn't yet grown dark, but the city lights were beginning to glow. I stared out over the city a moment. *Christina is out there somewhere.* I clenched a fist, remembering her bruised face. *How am I ever going to find her?*

My fingers drummed on the desk as the computer slowly opened. When the screen indicated all systems were working, I opened up a search engine. Delta Flight 1415 was the first thing I typed in. That seemed to be the most likely place to start. I was right. A whole page of articles about the kidnapped American showed on my screen.

I scanned through the tags, finally settling on a freshly-released AP article.

"American citizen held as collateral for stolen goods."

"Collateral for stolen goods?" I grated through a clenched jaw. "Christina is NOT collateral."

I scanned the article. It seemed to be a consensus among law enforcement officials that it was the work of the Japanese Mafia. There was a small, one-line quote from Brett Iverson. "We are praying for the safe return of our niece." That short sentence held a multitude of pain. I carried my own pain. *Her whole family is hurting,* I thought.

So...the Japanese Mafia. How did they get involved in all this? Then I remembered some overheard snippets of conversation over the past few weeks. I had dismissed them as rumors, but if they were brazenly kidnapping American citizens, the problem with the mafia was much bigger than I had imagined. *The peace treaty is creating desperation in their organization.* I reflected. *The mafia feeds on the hate in this region. If there is peace in the Middle East, the mafia will lose their demand for weapons. Israel has too long been a target for their greed.*

I knew the Japanese people well. I knew their customs. I knew their language. *How can this knowledge assist me now?*

Like every other young Israeli, I was a member of the National Guard. I had trained with military forces through my high school years. I knew how to use a gun just like every other Israeli citizen. But a gun wasn't my weapon of choice. Guns killed. *I don't want Christina dead.*

I stared at the computer screen unseeingly. The musings of my mind were what held my interest.

The flashing cursor caught my eye. Its insistent regularity reminded me of something my hand-to-hand combat instructor had told me.

"Real expertise comes from the calm, steady focus of your mind. Before you can train the body, you must learn to focus." I remembered his pause while he looked over the

166

assembled students. "Every single one of you can work a computer. Until the cursor is blinking steadily, no amount of pressure can get the computer to run even the simplest task. Think of your mind as the cursor. You must be able to clear your mind so you can focus on the task at hand." Benjamin Fischer had hinted at being connected with the secret service. Nothing we could have called him on, but enough to make us all suspicious. Approaching sixty, he wasn't a young man, but he was one of the best instructors I'd ever had.

I quickly typed in his name. There were a few short articles about different awards he'd won. After scanning through several pages on the search engine site, I finally came across a small article. "Benjamin Fischer, long-time instructor for the Israeli National Guard, retires." I scanned through the article. The journalist who had written the article had included an email address at the end. I quickly typed out a small note.

M. Abramson:

I am a former student of Benjamin Fischer and would like to get in touch with him. Do you have an email address where I can contact him?

Thanks for your help.

Todd Cohen

I sighed. The time between sending a letter and having it opened didn't have a precise measurement. *The only thing left for me to do is pray...and fast.*

A quiet knock at the door a few minutes later disturbed my troubled thoughts.

"Dinner." It was Father's voice.

I opened the door to look at his concerned face. "I won't be eating tonight."

"You need to keep your strength up."

"I'm fasting."

167

Father stared at me a moment then turned and headed down the hall to the kitchen. His refusal to argue was an unexpected surprise. My whole world was turning inside out. Nothing seemed familiar.

My door shut with a quiet *click*. I knelt by my bed to supplicate the Lord for the protection of Christina. Leaving her life in His hands was the only thing I could do.

I wandered back over to the computer to see if there was any more news on the Andrews case. Nothing. Not a surprise. I switched over to my email account and was surprised to see a response from Abramson. Hesitantly, I clicked on the "open" key. The note was cryptic, but it held the information I so desperately needed.

The email address for Benjamin Fischer is b.fischer@imi.mil.

I recognized the handle. Mil stood for military. *If he's retired, why does he still have a military email address?* I wondered. I quickly typed out another note:

Dear Benjamin Fischer:

I am a former student of yours. It's been five years since you trained me. I still remember most of the combat techniques you taught.

I spent two years in Japan learning their culture and language. Rumor has it that the Japanese Mafia kidnapped an American citizen today. Her name is Christina Andrews. Do you know anything about the case? If you do, is there any way I can help?

I stopped and stared at the screen a few moments, trying to figure out how to convey the importance of this request in only a few words. Finally, I continued.

Christina is a friend of mine from college. Her safety means more to me than I can express.

If you don't know anything about the case, could you please direct me to someone who does? Thanks for your response.
Todd Cohen

I pushed the send key and leaned back in my desk chair. Once again, I was back in the waiting game. It wasn't a game I liked.

Chapter 15, Prints

I spent the next couple of hours searching for anything that could give me a clue as to what the kidnappers might want. There was a redacted list of passengers in the AP article detailing the kidnapping. It listed passenger ages and nationalities.

There were people from all over the world on the flight. I ran my fingers through my hair. *How am I supposed to find clues from this?* I wondered in frustration. *There's nothing here to even hazard guesses.* I stared at the list again then clicked on an accompanying link.

How did the authorities decide the Japanese Mafia was involved in the crime? *They have more information than a seating chart.* I reminded myself. I'd only caught the tail end of the announcement. Quickly, I found the link to the evening news and listened to the replay of the earlier report. When Christina's bruised face flashed on the screen, my jaw clenched.

The droning voice of the reporter made its way past my rage. "American citizen, Christina Andrews, was kidnapped from her hotel room yesterday afternoon around four o'clock. A call claiming responsibility for the kidnapping came into our station earlier today. The call was traced to a cell phone purchased by a Hirohito Daisuki. A background check revealed ties to the Japanese Mafia. When police officers followed the cell phone signals, they found the disposable phone in a recycling bin not far from the intersections of Yitzchak Kariv and King David Street."

My eyes narrowed at that statement. I was familiar with that intersection. I couldn't imagine anyone just tossing a phone near there without someone noticing.

I sighed as I pictured the scene. If anyone had walked up and tossed something in a recycling bin, I had to admit I wouldn't have even been able to say whether it was a male or female, let alone any other detail. Mundane activities weren't alarming enough to create a clear memory. If I couldn't imagine myself remembering, how could I possibly expect anyone else to remember?

My mind snapped back to the subject at hand as the voice of the broadcaster continued, "The call was demanding the return of an item stolen two days ago from Delta Flight 1415 between the United States and Israel. If demands are not met within 72 hours, they will not guarantee the safety of Ms. Andrews."

I massaged my temples wearily. *What could possibly have been stolen? What did it have to do with Christina?* I stared at the passenger list again, head aching with the impossible task of deciphering clues.

As I stared at the list, a pocket of Japanese tourists just a few rows up from where Christina sat jumped out at me. The men were the only concentrated group of Japanese travelers on the plane. There were two other Japanese nationals, but they were sitting next to other nationalities on the flight. I wondered if these men might know something about what had been stolen.

I printed out the redacted list of passengers and the accompanying display of the assigned seats. After I circled the group of Japanese nationals, I readied myself for bed, turned off the lights and tried to sleep.

Images of Christina's battered face kept intruding. *Are they hurting her?* All the articles I'd read about sex trafficking by the Japanese Mafia replayed in my head. They prided themselves on their honorable behavior, but there was nothing honorable in forcing women into prostitution.

There had been some rumors, too, about honor killings. I shuddered. The men responsible for her kidnapping were not the type to care whether Christina lived or died.

My heart cried out in agony and I moved to the side of my bed, my head in my hands. I supplicated the Lord in anguished whispers for the safety of Christina. The pain of knowing she was in the hands of psychopathic men put a lie to my earlier pain. Thinking she was with Mark was a walk in the park compared to knowing she was in the hands of known criminals. If I had to repeat the last few weeks, I would've been on my knees begging the Lord to leave her in the loving arms of Mark.

I wasn't prepared for the searing pain that left me breathless. I stared up at the ceiling and whispered, "I can't do this. I just can't." I wiped the unfamiliar trickle of tears off my cheek.

Somehow, I was able to hear a still, small voice answer my pleas. "You don't have to. I am with you, always." Despite the fears I had thought insurmountable, I was able to relax and get some much-needed rest.

I awoke with a start and stared at the ceiling. Bright moonlight outlined the window. For a moment, I felt at peace with the world. Then I remembered another person who might be staring at moonlight framed in a different window. Christina.

I jumped out of bed and flipped on my computer. As it hummed to life, I glanced at the digital clock sitting by my bed. 5:09 a.m. The red numbers glared accusingly. I knew I had few hours of sleep, but the adrenaline was flowing through my veins. Sleep was not an option.

After an interminable amount of time, three minutes on the clock, my cursor blinked at me. I clicked on my internet connection and opened my email.

Shocked to see a reply from Benjamin Fischer, I stared at it a moment. Dread hit me. I was reluctant to open it. My throat was dry. With shaking fingers, I clicked on the email. I closed my eyes then opened them to read the contents.

Todd:

I remember you from the combat class. You were an exceptional student. You seemed to be able to clear your mind better than most of my students. I was impressed.

I don't know what lead you to contact me, but I am familiar with the Christina Andrews case. I've been asked to head the hunt for her captors. As you are apparently aware, the Japanese Mafia seems to be the likely group responsible. Your knowledge of the language will be a great asset.

If you are able, I'd like to have a meeting with you and a group of investigators at the scene of the crime.

I'm looking forward to working with you.

Ben

At the bottom of the email was a link to the hotel in question. I was familiar with the place. My parents had hosted a few banquets there for their numerous clients.

My palms were sweating as I stepped to the bathroom. Time was of the essence. I had no doubt that the Mafia was not bluffing. I didn't want to think about what might happen if her "guarantee" of protection ran out.

I moved as quietly as I could so I wouldn't wake Mother and Father. My shower lasted less than five minutes. If I hadn't been wide awake already, the icy blast from the shower head would've done the job. The brisk movement of the towel was hardly enough to dry my skin. I didn't notice. My focus was on getting Christina safely away from her captors.

I stepped back to my room and searched my closet for hiking boots, jeans, and a simple long-sleeved t-shirt. It seemed likely that I would need to be prepared for combat.

The hotel was only a few minutes away that time of day. Since it was still early when I arrived, I wasn't expecting anyone else from the investigative team. I was wrong. Benjamin Fischer, his short military cut almost hiding his gray, was already there speaking to the clerk behind the front desk.

He glanced my way when I entered and offered a curt nod before turning back to the clerk. She was handing him a key card as I joined him.

"You're early." Ben stated as he headed to the bank of elevators.

"I'm anxious to see this resolved, Sir."

"The rooms have been left as they were when Ms. Andrews was kidnapped other than the personal belongings of Mr. and Mrs. Iverson."

"Rooms?" I asked.

Ben nodded as the elevator doors opened on the top floor. "They had adjoining rooms. Mr. Iverson said it was so Ms. Andrews could have some privacy but still be able to care for the Iverson's infant."

"How old was the baby?" I asked.

"Three months."

"That's young for travelling."

"That's why they asked Ms. Andrews to travel with them. They didn't want to leave the baby in the States while they toured Jerusalem."

If only they had. I wished.

The room we entered was in disarray. The drawers had been pulled open and a few articles of clothing were strewn about. "I thought you said the Iversons took their belongings?" I asked.

"This was Ms. Andrews' room." Ben's voice was quietly respectful. It reminded me of how people speak at funerals, but this wasn't a funeral, and I wasn't going to give up until I knew Christina was safe.

The wardrobe doors were opened. I was surprised by the few clothes that hung there. *She wasn't planning any social events. This was clearly a working trip for her.* My brain couldn't help but wander into the forbidden zone. *Was she missing Mark?* I snapped myself out of that trap and glanced around the room. Christina's few scattered belongings didn't reveal anything.

We stepped to the dividing door between the two rooms. The wood had been splintered. Ben stooped to look at the damage on the door.

How was Christina feeling when this door failed? My throat constricted with fear for her.

We walked through the Iverson's suite. An eBook reader was on a nightstand next to a leather chair. Between the chair and a king-sized bed sat a portable crib. I wondered if it was Christina who had been reading. Had she been startled and put it down, or had Mrs. Iverson been reading it the night before? *If they took their belongings, this must be Christina's.*

As we headed toward the door, Ben bent down to investigate something on the floor. I joined him. A chalk outline of a gun was clearly drawn. I stepped back as if a snake had bitten me. The evidence of a weapon sent a shock through my system. Seeing Christina on the evening news had been difficult. Seeing the outline of a weapon sitting on the floor slapped me with its harsh reality.

"When the other investigators get here, they should have a fingerprint report." Ben muttered.

We both stared at the outline a moment. It was a few inches away from the door toward the far wall. Ben stooped to look at the door. He pointed at a small indentation on the wood. "Looks like it hit here."

Christina must've fought. What happened with the gun? Was she hit with it? How did she get the bruise on her face? Questions swirled through my mind.

The movie in my mind stopped abruptly when three men walked through the door. Two of them wore the uniform of the local police. The third was Israeli military. The taller officer handed a folder to Ben. "Here are the reports you requested."

Ben scanned them then stopped to peruse a particular page. "Interesting."

My eyebrows lifted in a question. Ben glanced up at me.

"There were different fingerprints on the barrel than the handle."

"What does that mean?"

"It means," Ben caught my eyes, "that someone wrestled the gun from someone else."

"Do you think Ms. Andrews held the gun?"

"Neither set of prints is in our national computer banks. We're having to go international. That takes a few more hours."

My heart constricted. Until the prints could be matched, the owner of the gun was in question. Any outsider bringing a gun into the country would be sent to prison. It wasn't a crime Israel took lightly. I closed my eyes and blew out a breath then stared at Ben.

"I doubt a young American in charge of an infant would be carrying a gun." Ben put a comforting hand on

177

my shoulder. "This isn't something you need to worry about."

While Ben conferred with the other two men, I wandered toward the folding crib. A leather strap was poking out from underneath. My heart gave a jolt. *Christina's purse.* I'd seen it before. I glanced at the conversing men then bent down to pull out her purse.

Ben walked over as I dumped the contents onto the bed. Her wallet, makeup, a few coins, a small pack of wipes, and a cell phone tumbled out. My brows furrowed as I reached for the phone. "I don't remember her owning a phone like this..." My voice trailed off. The now-open phone trailed Japanese characters across the screen.

Ben looked over my shoulder. "What does it say?"

"Carpe diem."

His brows drew together in a puzzled frown. "What kind of label is that?"

I shrugged and put in a few tries at passwords—all the factory ones. It was surprising how many people didn't ever bother to change from a standard password. None of them worked.

Ben moved over and stared at the phone while I attempted to get a correct password. I knew five wrong tries would get the phone locked up for a few hours. I offered a silent prayer then remembered the Latin phrase that completed "Carpe Diem." A feeling of grave importance hung over me. Whatever information this phone held was the key to free Christina. I was sure of it. Slowly, I keyed in the words "Quam Minimum Credula Postero." An open phone was my reward. I let out my held breath and scanned the items on the screen.

The first was a list of contacts. Nothing unusual. The names weren't familiar, but I hadn't expected them to be. I'd had no contact with the mafia during my stay in Japan. They didn't interact much with law-abiding citizens, and missionaries didn't have contact with the Japanese underworld.

Besides, I had no idea if the contact names were real or just pseudonyms.

Ben was staring over my shoulder. "How did you find the password?"

I continued to scroll through the phone while I answered, "How familiar are you with the line from Horace?"

"Horace who?"

"The Latin poet who is credited with creating the term Carpe Diem?"

"Not...but what does this have to do with..." Ben swallowed nervously, "this?"

"The line from Horace's poem is 'reap the day; trust not in tomorrow.' It seemed to make sense to try the next part of the phrase to unlock the phone. Whoever set this up seems to know Latin."

Ben was almost close enough to touch me as he stared over my shoulder. "The only people I know who study Latin these days are those in the medical field." Switching gears, he asked, "Did Christina speak Japanese?"

I shook my head. "I don't think so. She struggled with Spanish. I don't remember her ever saying anything about Japanese, and I know she hasn't been out of the country."

"What would she be doing with a phone full of Japanese contacts?"

I was skimming through the messages as dread filled me. "Give me a minute, please." I spent a couple of minutes scanning through the notes. A rock settled in my stomach. *This is bigger than me. It's bigger than Christina. What are the chances that this phone landed in my lap? How many other Israeli soldiers speak fluent Japanese?* I looked at Ben. By his expression, I could see he recognized the horror in my eyes. "This...is a plan for a...weapons deployment, but it's not the kind of weapon you'd expect."

Ben stared hard at the Japanese characters. "What are you talking about?"

"Biological warfare."

Silence. The three other men in the room had stopped their conversation and were staring at us in shock. Finally, Ben broke it, his voice breaking, "Biological warfare?"

I glanced at the other men then back at the phone. "There is no tomorrow for anyone who gets this disease. Carpe Diem. Reap the day." I paused again, unwilling to be the bearer of bad news but knowing I had no choice. "The seeds have been planted. All they need to do is harvest."

Ben's voice sounded impatient. "What do you mean?"

"According to these notes, this has been planned for years. It's in our food supply, GMOs, genetically modified organisms—specifically, genetically modified yeast. We've been warned and forewarned. The GMOs we've been eating have changed our chemical makeup. A disease that wouldn't have even created a cold just fifteen years ago has the power to wipe out whole populations—especially those who rely almost exclusively on mass-produced goods."

"So this isn't just about Israel, is it?" Ben was subdued.

"No, Sir, it has the potential to impact the entire planet."

"The mafia is ready to release it because... they are the sole possessor of the antibody. Do you know how much people will pay to survive?" I couldn't hide the strain in my voice.

"How are they going to accomplish this?"

"It doesn't take much to set off a disease. Just a few vials can infect the whole country. The vials are stored in a case inside a locker. This phone," I stared at it in horror, "has the code to unlock the case for the release of the vials.

There are people from all over the planet here this week. You've seen the crowds." The other men nodded. "All they have to do is release this in the air. The people here will do the rest." I looked down at the notes so carelessly abandoned. "The incubation period is two weeks. Most of those infected won't even know they're sick until it's too late."

I stared at the phone as if it was going to explode. *Is there any hope?*

Chapter 16, Passover

B en stared at me a moment. "You say this... disease... is linked to yeast?"

I nodded, unable to speak.

A slow smile spread across Ben's face. "The Mafia has made a mistake in their planning."

"What do you mean?" My brow furrowed in confusion.

"This is the week of Passover." He paused to wait for recognition to register.

Suddenly hopeful, I broke in, "Faithful Jewish homes have no yeast."

Ben nodded.

"There is hope."

"While God lives, there is always hope." Ben gripped my arm then released it and turned to the other three men in the room. "This information needs to be handled through the proper channels. I trust you know what to do."

They nodded curtly and turned on their heels.

Ben turned back to me. "Our job now is to find Christina and her kidnappers. They will know where this locker is. A weapon this dangerous should not be left in the hands of criminals. We have a few leads, but I'm not sure which ones to follow."

Ben pulled out his smart phone and scrolled to his notes. I looked over his shoulder as he scanned through the documents. Staring hard at the screen, Ben asked, "You are familiar with the Japanese culture. Where do you think we should go?"

I cleared my throat, "I'm not familiar with the criminal element, Sir. The people I worked with were law-abiding citizens."

Ben's phone showed a map of Jerusalem and the purported hideouts the Mafia had used in the past. I stared at the screen and prayed. *We have no time. Please help us.* Three of the hideouts were within walking distance of the recycling can where the phone had been located.

I pointed at the one closest to the can. "Let's try here."

Ben quickly called for backup. When we stepped out of the hotel, a sedan with tinted windows met us at the curb.

The opening door revealed three Israeli soldiers equipped with submachine guns. My heart dropped. *Guns mean death. I don't want Christina in the crossfire.* Swallowing my fear, I scrambled in behind Ben. We rode in silence to the hideout.

We stopped in a dirty alleyway. The narrow alley could hardly fit the sedan. Two of the soldiers jumped out and stood next to the door, weapons at ready. The third soldier jumped out and kicked in the door. The other two followed the first, their guns aimed at the inhabitants.

Ben and I followed quickly. There were two women and five men in the room, in various stages of dress. Their eyes were wide in shock and horror. I scanned the faces. They looked oriental. None of them was a face I wanted to see. Christina was not in the room. One of the soldiers remained in the room, his gun aimed at the shocked inhabitants, while the other two soldiers carefully searched the rest of the apartment. They came back a few minutes later, shaking their heads.

When I spoke, all eyes were on me. I knew my Japanese was flawless. "Where is the girl? The American?"

They all stood, stone silent. One of the soldiers took my slight nod as encouragement and moved to the man who seemed to be in charge. The soldier shoved his gun into his face. I asked, "Who is in charge?"

Sweat poured down the man's face, but he refused to talk. The other soldier slapped one of the cowering men.

"We know about the vials. You will die here. All of you. Unless you tell me who I need to talk to."

The honor code of the mafia wasn't enough to convince the man he wanted to die. He blurted out that he wasn't the leader, the leader wasn't there and then told us his leader's name, then shut down when the others grunted in protest. The name was all I needed. The Israeli military already had the places located.

A couple of military vehicles were pulling up as Ben and I walked out the door. I looked at Ben, a question in my eyes. "They will be arrested. We've been watching them for months. We couldn't figure out what they were doing until you stumbled on their plan."

I nodded and we headed to the next place on the list, the three soldiers crowding into the sedan with us. Once again, we were silent, all lost in our own thoughts. *I wonder if the soldiers are reconciling with their God over potentially taking a human life.* My eyes travelled over their deadly weapons. *Please, God,* I prayed, *please protect Christina.*

The next place on our list was a warehouse. The soldiers played the previous scene through again, jumping out and assuming position, then bursting through the door. This time, the routine yielded an empty room. It had been cleared out.

Ben and I wandered through the small warehouse. I stopped and pulled out the phone that had caused so much heartache and stared at it a moment.

As I stared at the phone, I asked. "How do you think they found Christina?"

Ben glanced up at me. In unison, we said, "A phone tracer."

I scrambled through the apps on the phone until I found the tracer. A few clicks later and a location for a different phone was flashing on the screen. I glanced at Ben.

"If I remember right, this next place is right on a busy thoroughfare. Unless you want the whole country in an uproar, we can't burst in the same way we've done the last two times. What do you recommend?"

He pursed his lips. "With your linguistic skills, you might be able to talk yourself in. The soldiers can be backup if we need them. They can follow in a separate car."

I nodded. "That will have to do. Let's go."

Christina

The air from the opening door swept cold across my face, waking me in an instant. I sat up and cringed against the far wall, uncertain what Demon wanted.

He sneered and jerked his thumb toward the door, indicating where he wanted me. I scrambled to stand, not taking time to brush the wrinkles out of my shirt, hoping my empty belly would refrain from its constant complaining.

As I entered the room, the men were speaking quickly in a tongue I couldn't hope to understand. Their glances my direction didn't look friendly. I shrunk against the wall and wished it would swallow me. *How did I ever get into this mess?* I wondered for the hundredth time. *And how do I get out of it?* The next thought was directed heavenward, *Please, Father, guide me and help me escape.*

One of the men walked over to me and displayed a phone. My brows knit together in confusion and then opened wide in understanding. When he saw the look in my eyes, he asked in broken English. "See this you?"

Hesitantly, I nodded.

"What pwace?"

"The airplane."

"It you wiff?"

I shook my head, my long curls swinging back and forth, echoing my certainty. *I left the phone on the plane.* My brows wrinkled in confusion. Suddenly, an image of me falling into the wall of the bathroom and then stuffing my wipes in my purse filled my mind. *Where did that phone go?* I wondered. Then I remembered I hadn't heard the phone drop. *Had it landed in my purse? Wouldn't I have noticed?* I bit my lip and remembered how sick I'd been and the loud buzzing of the alarm. *I wouldn't have noticed if a whole boatload had dropped.* My brown eyes must've revealed my swirling thoughts.

The interrogator's eyes narrowed, and he raised a threatening fist. I cowered and bit back a whimper. "Whel phone?"

I could hardly form the words in my terror. "May-maybe in my purse?"

Angrily, the interrogator turned to my kidnapper. This time, he spoke in broken English, intending for me to hear. "Why no you get phone?"

My kidnapper ducked his head in shame. "Beacon wed me to woom her, but no find. Awarm set she."

My eyes widened at the realization that my setting off the alarm had interrupted his quest for the phone. Had I not set off an alarm, he might've picked up the phone and left.

A chill ran through me. I gripped my hands under my folded arms to hide their trembling.

The arm that had so recently been lifted at me made contact with the cowering man. I couldn't watch. I closed my eyes tight until I heard the interrogator speak again.

"Whel pulse you?"

"At-at" I couldn't prevent the break in my voice. "the hotel."

"Nevel mind." His face took on an evil twist. "Soon find we."

I swallowed hard. *Please, Father, help Tina, Brett, and Connor to stay out of this. Please keep them safe.*

I jumped when three quick raps sounded at the door. Three more followed in quick succession. My interrogator asked something in a foreign tongue. It was answered quickly, and my interrogator cautiously opened the door.

A whiff of a familiar fragrance had me examining the visitor. He was wearing a hat pulled low and sunglasses and was speaking quickly to the five men in the room. It sounded angry and low. I had no way of understanding. Despite the dire circumstances and his angry tone, I felt peace replace the terror in my heart.

Without understanding the exchange of words, I understood the movement when the stranger reached for my arm. "Come you me with." I glanced at the stranger and tried not to show my shock. *Todd? Todd here? But how? And why?*

He jerked me roughly out the door. I stumbled after him to a waiting car, its windows darkened. I had no idea where we were going, but I was with Todd, and nothing else mattered.

As we were driving away, Todd pulled off his hat and glasses, then reached over to gently caress my bruised face. "Christina, I'm so glad you're alive." I could hear the joy in his voice, then his tone changed to one of concern. "Does this hurt?"

"It's a little tender." I threw my arms around him and hugged him like I'd never let him go. "I've never been so happy to see someone in my life." His returning hug was fierce, then he tenderly touched my bruised face. I fought a desire to turn my head and kiss his exploring fingers, but I wanted some answers. "How did you find me?"

"The Israeli military got involved the minute the news was out. I volunteered to help." His gentle fingers were still caressing my face as he continued, "We didn't find you at first. I didn't think you had much time." His eyes sparkled with unshed tears. "I prayed and then the thought occurred to me that if there was a beacon to find the phone which led them to you, it could probably be put in reverse. So that's what I did. And it worked."

His thumb was gently caressing my lips. I closed my eyes at the overwhelming feelings his gentle fingers created. When he moved on to toy with my tangled curls, I could concentrate enough to ask, "But how did you get in without a fight?"

"The first place we visited gave us the name of the leader here in Israel. It was crucial information. One of my investigators once said that if he closed his eyes while I was speaking, he couldn't have told the difference between me and a native-born speaker. My delivery was flawless." I reached up to wipe his tear that had spilled over while he continued. "It had to be. Your life depended on it. As far as they know, I've taken you to the leader in the city until the phone is properly located."

Todd looked down at me with such tenderness my breath caught. After a moment of silence, his husky voice continued, "So...I got your note."

I couldn't stop the tears then. He held me to his chest and let me cry. An angry protest from my empty stomach stopped the tears. A hiccup escaped and we both giggled then laughed. Todd put his arm around me as I rested my head on his chest. "Hungry?"

I nodded. "Starving."

"There's no CougarEat in Israel, but I think I can find something suitable. How would you like to meet my parents?"

I pushed back and stared at him. His expression warmed my heart. It was full of such love and tenderness, I had to ask, "Does that mean something?"

He nodded. "I hope it does. I was going to wait and court you properly, but almost losing you nearly sent me over the edge." He gently cupped my face. "Christina, Darling, would you honor me with your hand in marriage?"

The tears that had stopped suddenly started up again. "I know this sounds crazy, but after I broke up with Mark, I couldn't get you out of my mind." I smiled up at him through my tears. The peace that filled my soul was an answer to a question I knew I didn't have to ask. The answer was in my heart. A forever changed one. "Yes, Todd, yes."

With that answer, he bent down to touch his lips softly to mine. His gentle lips moved over the bruises on my face, barely touching the injured skin. My skin tingled with desire for his touch.

"Ah, Christina, I have lived through a living nightmare. It is one I never want to live through again."

I suddenly pulled back.

"What is it?" His brows drew together in a puzzled frown.

I bit my lip. "I don't know how to say this. I hope it comes out right." I stared out the tinted glass a moment and peeked at the driver who was ignoring all the activity in the back seat. I glanced up at Todd and prayed I wouldn't hurt him. "I...I just can't raise my children in a war zone."

He pulled back, a hurt look replacing the puzzled one. "What are you saying? You won't marry me?"

I bit my lip again, unsure of how to proceed. "I just can't live in Israel. I'm sorry. I want my children raised in the United States." Images of my carefree childhood spilled into my mind. It was a childhood I wanted to share with my children.

"It is decided then." His voice sounded almost cheerful. I stared up at him. *Did he hear what I said?* "My parents own an accounting firm in New York. They need another partner there. Would that suit you?"

"New York?" *I was thinking more of Salina, Kansas. But you go where the job is...* Then I remembered how thrilled I was to fly over New York and see the Statue of Liberty. "Would we live in the City?"

"I can commute." He was quick to answer. "I'd expect you'd want to live in a house?"

I nodded, speechless. *This man thinks of everything.* Tired of talking, I pulled his face to meet mine. This time, I wasn't settling for a timid exploration.

A short drive brought us to a newer subdivision on the outskirts of Jerusalem. A couple in their mid-forties were standing at the door when we arrived.

Joyfully, Todd led me to them. "Mother, Father, this is Christina Andrews."

"We're so glad you're safe. We've been praying for you."

I reached out to grasp his mother's offered hand. "I felt your prayers, and I know my family prayed too." Suddenly thinking of them, I asked, "Would it be alright if I called my parents? I want to let them know I'm safe."

"Of course." Todd's mother led me to their phone and I quickly dialed.

After what seemed like an eternity, just three short rings, the phone was picked up. "Hello?"

I could hear all the pain and anxiety in Mom's voice. "Hi, Mom, it's me, Christina."

She gasped. "Are you okay?"

"Yes, Mom. Todd found me." I looked up at the man whose hands were lightly resting on my shoulders. I wanted the connection as much as he did.

Her voice broke as she held back a grateful sob. "Thanks for calling, Sweetie. We've been so worried. Have you called Tina and Brett yet?"

I shook my head, then remembered she couldn't see. "No. I don't have my cell phone and I don't have their number memorized."

"I can take care of it for you. When will you be back in the States?"

My brows furrowed. "I'm not sure. I really don't feel like doing any sightseeing now." I couldn't help trembling, the memory of the past hours engulfing me. Todd's hands gently squeezed my shoulders, as if assuring me he was there. "I'd like to get home as quickly as possible."

"We want you home." She paused a moment, the air heavy with unasked questions. Finally, she said, "You can fill me in on the details when you get here." I was grateful for Mom's insight. I couldn't bring myself to reliving the past just then. I didn't want to melt into a puddle of tears in front of Todd's parents, and I knew reliving the past would push me past my reserves.

After a simple dinner with no yeast—Todd explained about the preparations for the Passover—he made arrangements to fly back to the United States. He also called the police. I would have to give a report, but Todd assured me he would be with me. I needed his support.

The next morning, we walked hand in hand through the airport terminal in Tel Aviv. I dropped his hand and raced to Aunt Tina when I saw her tear-streaked face. "We're so sorry we put you through this, Christina. We had no idea there was any danger."

"It wasn't your fault. There wasn't anything you could do." I paused and smiled up at Todd, who had quickly joined us. "If things hadn't happened exactly the way they had, Todd wouldn't have been able to read what was on the phone." I shuddered. "Who knows what horrible disease would even now be ravaging the world."

Todd reached out to envelope his warm hand around mine. "God does very often interfere in all our lives for good." He stooped down to kiss the top of my head. "And I'm very grateful he does."

I sighed happily. "So am I." Then I laughed. "And I'm going to be ecstatic to be back in the good ole USA."

Tina and Brett joined in my laughter and all five of us, Connor sucking his fist, headed into the waiting plane.

Chapter 17, Permission

Peppy bounded up to the front gate as Todd pushed it open. His big paws landed on Todd's chest and Peppy's tongue left a wet glistening stripe up the side of his face. Laughing, Todd pushed the enormous black and white Great Dane down. "Easy boy. I've already had my bath today."

My heart soared at Peppy's happy greeting. This had been the kind of reception I'd expected when I brought Mark home. Apparently, Peppy was a better judge of character than I was.

"Peppy. Bad boy. Down." I tried unsuccessfully to scold the big dog. He knew me too well.

Peppy's long tail beat a rhythm against his side. I rubbed his face enthusiastically. "It's good to see you, Boy."

Tobias, Coby, Mary, Julie, and Nathan rushed out the door to join us. "Hi, Christina." Their voices rang in unison. Mom followed at a slower pace. Dad probably wasn't home from work yet.

Todd tossed a delighted Tobias in the air. When he settled Tobias back on the ground, he reached down to muss Coby's light brown curls. "Hey ya, Buddy. How's it going?"

"I kicked a home run in recess today."

Todd raised his eyebrows in a question. "Kicked?"

"Yeah. We were playing kickball."

"What's that?"

I looked up at him in wonder. "You don't know what kickball is?"

He shook his head. "Never heard of it."

Coby took over. "It's like baseball only instead of hitting a baseball with a stick, you kick a bouncy ball about the size of a volleyball. It's a lot of fun." He smiled up at Todd. "I always get picked first."

Todd chuckled. "That must mean you're a good player."

Coby nodded enthusiastically before Julie interrupted. "I always get picked first too. I'm in second grade. Coby is in third, so we don't have recess at the same time."

Todd struggled to keep a straight face. "It's a good thing you don't play at the same time. Coby wouldn't want to beat his sister at kickball."

"I wouldn't mind." Coby was adamant.

Julie stuck a small pink tongue at him, then turned to run back towards Mom, who had stopped on the porch steps while we were accosted by the crew. "I'm telling."

I giggled. "Welcome to the Andrews home."

Todd put his arm around my waist and gave it a small squeeze. "I can see why you miss your family so much."

I nodded. "Never a dull moment, that's for sure." I paused and glanced up at him. "Not that we've had many dull moments." I shuddered. "I'd rather not repeat the past few days."

"Me, too." His voice was fervent. He bent down to kiss the top of my head. "Although I'm grateful for the end result."

I smiled up at him then reached for his hand. We walked the last few steps to the porch. I let go of Todd to envelope my mom in a hug. "I love you, Mom. I've missed you."

Tears glistened in her eyes. "I've missed you, too, Honey. We were so worried about you." She stepped back and touched my face gently. "You look a lot better than you did on television. Does it hurt much?"

I shook my head, my eyes misting over.

Mom looked up at Todd. "This must be..."

"Todd. Todd Cohen." He stepped forward and shook Mom's hand firmly. "I'm glad to finally meet you." He dropped her hand and reached for mine. "Christina spent a lot of time over the past couple of days talking about you. She really missed you."

Mom reached up to wipe a glistening tear from her eye. She cleared her throat so she could talk. Her voice was husky with unshed tears. "Dad is on his way. He had a meeting with a particularly difficult client today. It was a session he didn't think he should miss. We'll have dinner in about half an hour. Is that okay?"

We both nodded and followed Mom inside. It felt strange to enter through the front room since I was accustomed to entering through the kitchen. Peppy whined at the door. He knew he couldn't come in, but he wasn't above begging.

The oak floors glistened, their warm honey gold tint almost matching the shade of Mom's hair. Mom directed us to sit on one of the couches usually reserved for home teachers. The white upholstery wasn't something Mom let the kids use.

We settled on the white cushions. I sat at the edge of the seat, my legs crossed at the ankles. Suddenly, I remembered a similar pose when I'd been waiting for Mark to arrive for our first date. I had butterflies flitting in my tummy that night too. This time, I wasn't worried about impressing my date. It was impressing my dad I was worried about.

When Dad walked in, Todd jumped up to greet him. He held out his hand, and Dad gripped it in a firm handshake. He was sizing up Todd.

From his expression, I could tell he was impressed. He already knew the important stuff. He knew Todd would do whatever needed done to make sure I was safe. He'd proved it.

Todd turned and reached for my hand. I stood up next to him. We faced Dad together, a team already. "I guess you know why I'm here." I was surprised to feel sweat on his hand. I glanced up at him. He must be nervous. I hadn't thought he was the type.

Dad's twinkling eyes showed his amusement. "I can hazard a guess, but why don't you tell me?"

"I wanted to ask your permission to marry your daughter."

Dad was enjoying the moment. Mark hadn't bothered to ask. "Well, since you're asking, I have a question in return."

Todd swallowed. Facing my dad was harder on him than I thought it would be. "Yes, Sir."

"Where were you planning to marry her?"

"We'd discussed several options, but we thought the Kansas City Temple would work out the best for our families, Sir."

Dad grinned. "Sounds like you have it all planned out. You have my—our blessing." He paused to seek out Mom, who was standing in the doorway. He stepped to her side and took her hand, then turned to face us. "We're delighted to have you join the family. And you can call us Mom and Dad Andrews, if you like."

I stepped over to hug Dad. "Thanks, Dad. I love you."

He hugged me back, a tight embrace that communicated all the anguish I knew he'd felt when I'd been missing. It must have been agonizing for them.

As they turned to the kitchen, I blurted out, "Is there time for a quick tour of the house before dinner?"

Mom turned to stare at me a moment. "We have about ten more minutes before dinner is done." She bit her lip, a sign of her indecision, then she said, "Go ahead, but it's at your own risk. I'm not sure how clean the bedrooms are. They're beyond my inspection zone."

I snickered. "So are we talking knee deep in dirty laundry?"

"Something like that." She smiled and headed back to the kitchen, where the delightful scents of roast beef and baked potatoes mingled with the smell of fresh baked rolls. I thought I detected a hint of cinnamon and baked apples. Mom made the best apple pie I'd ever tasted. She knew it was my favorite. My mouth watered. It had been months since I'd tasted Mom's cooking.

I tugged lightly at Todd's hand. "Let's go."

He followed me up the wide spiral staircase to the second floor. "This is Mom and Dad's room, the main bathroom, the girl's room, and Dad's study."

We moved to the straight staircase that led to the third floor. "The boys share a room upstairs. My old room is up there too." We walked up the narrow stairs, the ancient wood protesting our movements with angry squeaks. I giggled and turned to wrinkle my nose at him. "We couldn't ever play hide and seek in the house. The floors gave our steps away."

Todd grinned. "That could be a problem."

He followed me quietly as I opened the solid oak door leading to my bedroom. It was a large airy room. He stopped in the doorway, respecting my need to experience my childhood space alone.

I stepped over to the window overlooking the yard and pressed my forehead against the cool glass. The waves in the glass blurred the outside world. I had always loved the old glass. It held secret memories of other girls who had looked through it in the century since it had been created.

199

There were only a few panes of the old glass left in the house. I hoped the glass in my window would last another lifetime.

As I stared into the yard, images of working in the garden with Dad, mowing the large yard, swinging in the old tire swing that hung from a towering cottonwood, and playing tag with my brothers and sisters flashed through my mind. My childhood had come and gone. Was I really ready to leave it all behind? Todd moved quietly across the room. He put his arm around my shoulders. "Nice view."

I nodded then tilted my face to his. When his lips met mine, warm and tender, my heart raced with joyous anticipation. Suddenly, I felt as if I was standing beside myself. I wasn't who I'd been. I was a daughter of a living God, who loved me. The man who raped my mother did not define me. Todd's warm lips on mine brought with them a feeling of peace and assurance. I might be losing my childhood, but the future with Todd in it looked bright, indeed.

About the Author

*R*oseanne E. Wilkins, the author of the popular Kansas Connections Series, was raised surrounded by the open wheat fields of Kansas. She majored in elementary education while attending BYU. After marrying Craig, they moved around the country for several years. Before they had children, she spent spare moments writing but put her writing aside when her first son was born. That was 1991. In 2008, she was moved to write a fanfiction book, *Noonday Sun*. After finishing the fanfiction, she found several old manuscripts which she intends to finish—even if it takes another 20 years to do it. She loves to hear from her readers. You can reach her at rewilkins9@msn.com or read more on her blog at www.RoseannesSpot.blogspot.com.

Author's Note

Thﬁ his book is a work of fiction. I don't believe there is a disease out there capable of doing what my book implies. However, I do think it's important for each of us to learn the laws of health and apply them in our lives.

I've had this novel pretty much finished since July of 2011. Since that time, I've had the opportunity to get to know Caleb Warnock, best-selling author of *Forgotten Skills of Self-Sufficiency Used by the Mormon Pioneers*, and the co-author of his new book, Melissa Richardson. Caleb and Melissa's book on breads and natural yeasts, *The Art of Baking with Natural Yeast: Breads, Pancakes, Waffles, Cinnamon Rolls and Muffins*, is available on-line and at any book store. Because of Caleb's interest in natural yeasts and my knowledge of current events regarding genetically-modified organisms (GMOs), I decided to include a little bit about them in my book. I wanted to take a moment to thank Caleb for his willingness to share his insight with the rest of us.

I also wanted to thank Gayle Boyd, who graciously agreed to my mentioning her wonderful book in my own. Although there are no new copies available, I found her book, *Days of Awe*, to be full of information designed to benefit any LDS home.

Made in the USA
Las Vegas, NV
26 April 2024